The passengers and crew of a Lufthansa flight from Ankara to Hamburg are feared dead following a plane crash in Romania. The Boeing 747, which was carrying three hundred and sixty-two passengers, lost altitude thirty minutes after take-off and came down close to the Bicaz Gorge in the north-east of the country. A spokesperson from the Ministry for Foreign Affairs has confirmed that there were five Swedish citizens on board.

* * *

A young Swedish girl has miraculously been found alive following the recent plane crash in Romania. According to rescue workers at the scene, she was airlifted to hospital in Timișoara on Sunday morning and is understood to be in a critical condition.

Rescue operations continue in the inaccessible Bicaz Gorge, but the likelihood of finding any more survivors is thought to be very small.

A
PLAY
TO
KILL

Alex Ahndoril is a new pseudonym for the writers behind Lars Kepler, Alexandra and Alexander Ahndoril. Lars Kepler is a No.1 bestselling international sensation, whose Joona Linna thrillers have sold more than 17 million copies in 40 languages.

A
PLAY
TO
KILL

ALEX AHNDORIL

ZAFFRE

Originally published in Sweden by Albert Bonniers Förlag in 2024
This edition published in the UK in 2026 by
ZAFFRE
An imprint of Bonnier Books UK 5th Floor,
HYLO, 105 Bunhill Row, London, EC1Y 8LZ

Published by agreement with Salomonsson Agency
Translation copyright © 2026 by Alice Menzies

A CIP catalogue record for this book is available from the British Library.

Hardback ISBN: 978-1-80418-733-3
Trade paperback ISBN: 978-1-80418-734-0

Also available as an ebook and an audiobook

1 3 5 7 9 10 8 6 4 2

Typeset by IDSUK (Data Connection) Ltd
Printed and bound by CPI (UK) Ltd, Croydon CR0 4YY

The authorised representative in the EEA is Bonnier Books
UK (Ireland) Limited.
Registered office address: Floor 3, Block 3, Miesian Plaza,
Dublin 2, D02 Y754, Ireland
compliance@bonnierbooks.ie
www.bonnierbooks.co.uk

One

SITTING ACROSS FROM HER EX-HUSBAND Sidney Mendelson at a table at Ekstedt in central Stockholm, Julia Stark sipped her wine as she waited for their next course to arrive.

Soft flickers of warm light danced across the floors and walls from the birch logs burning in the hearth.

Two weeks ago, Julia had turned to Sid for help on a case for the first time. He took a few days' leave from his job with Norrmalm Police and travelled to the forests of Västernorrland with her.

In a moment of playful overconfidence, Julia had bet Sid that she would be able to solve the case at Mannheim within four days and, as a result, had cut corners and made a number of serious mistakes that she still felt embarrassed about. But despite all that, she had won the bet.

That was why he had invited her out to dinner this evening.

Julia often fantasised about Sid wanting to work with her again, possibly even becoming a partner in Stark Detective Agency, but hadn't drummed up the courage to ask him yet.

This was the first time they had been out to eat together since their divorce three years ago, and Julia was trying her best to be fully present, to enjoy these few short hours together.

She kept reminding herself not to ask any more of him, but of course it happened all the same.

'Would you consider having dinner with me again?' she heard herself ask.

He looked up, and she immediately regretted her question when she saw the hesitation in his eye.

'Every once in a while,' she clarified. 'No more than that . . .'

'I'd love to,' he said, reaching out and putting a warm hand on top of hers.

'You don't have to if you don't w—'

'I do.'

'There was actually one more thing. If I need your help again, professionally . . .'

'We'll see,' he said with a smile.

His reply made her eyes well up, and she was on the verge of saying something she would probably regret when she heard her phone ping in her bag. Julia mumbled an apology, took out her mobile, read the message and looked up.

'Do you know the actress Bianca Salo?' she asked.

'Of course. I saw her as Puck not too long ago,' he replied. 'Why?'

Julia felt a warmth spread across her chest, and she couldn't stop herself from smiling.

'She wants to hire Stark Detective Agency.'

'Did she say why?'

Julia nodded. 'She says her dead fiancé is stalking her.'

'OK . . .' he said. 'That sounds a bit . . .'

'I know.'

'Like serious paranoia. Paranoid psychosis or something.'

'I know, but what if it's not? Imagine,' she said with a smile.

They were quiet for a moment, mumbling a subdued thank you when the waiter arrived with two plates of charred turbot and sugar snap peas on an artful spiral of orange sauce.

By the time they left the restaurant, the August sky was dark. The rain had stopped while they were eating, but the streets were still wet, the air cool and fresh.

As ever, Julia gripped Sid's arm and leaned against the cane in her other hand as they crossed Östermalmstorg.

She often joked that she was actually pretty good-looking as long as it wasn't windy, but with him she had always felt beautiful no matter the weather.

Julia was thirty-three, with strawberry blonde colouring, dark green eyes and a straight nose. She typically used her hair to cover the deep scar on her cheek, but if a gust of wind happened to blow it back from her face, she let it happen.

They stopped to let a couple of cars pass on Sibyllegatan.

There was a man standing in the shadows on the steps up to the cemetery, and Julia felt a knot of anxiety in the pit of her stomach when she thought she saw him push out his lower lip and draw a line of tears down one cheek. She quickly pulled Sid over to the other side of the road to stop him from noticing the man and tried to tell herself that it was all in her mind.

When she was eighteen, a journalist at one of the tabloids had published a piece about the lavish life she was living on her compensation and inherited money. The very same day, on social media, someone had posted a photograph of Julia grieving her family alongside one of her laughing, captioning the image: *Two seconds later.*

Hundreds of more and less imaginative versions of that post were shared around the world, and the meme briefly went viral before vanishing into the ether like some sort of toy people were bored of.

Julia had never forgotten just how quickly and easily a cruel joke could tip over into hatred and outright victimisation, and she still found it incredibly painful when people claimed that she acted sad whenever anyone was looking, but started living life to the full the minute they turned their back.

During that brief period, she had become a poster girl for hypocrisy. Her sad face appeared alongside politicians talking about climate change, or religious leaders claiming that all lives were of equal value.

Years had now passed, but Julia still avoided social media and occasionally found herself panicking if she happened to laugh in public.

She was now walking down Storgatan beside Sid, listening to him enthusiastically comparing the jazz pianists Bill Evans and Esbjörn Svensson.

She had put the embarrassment and unease behind her.

Julia tried to walk slowly in order to make the moment last longer, resting her head against his shoulder as though she was tired.

'Are you OK?' asked Sid.

'Fine,' she mumbled.

The sound of their footsteps and her cane echoed softly between the buildings.

A number of flattened cardboard boxes and blankets had been left in a doorway.

'I had a great time this evening,' she said.

'Me too,' Sid replied quietly.

Around the signpost by the pedestrian crossing, a broken bicycle wheel hung from its cable lock. On the back of the sign, Julia noticed, there was a sticker of a watchful doe. She had seen several of them dotted around the city lately.

They crossed the street and turned off towards the water. In one of the windows they passed, a man stood watching them from behind a lace curtain.

Julia would have loved for their walk to go on all night, but they had already reached her door at Styrmansgatan 15.

A lock of hair fell over her forehead, and she pushed it back behind her ear, steadied herself using her cane and looked up.

As she met Sid's warm eyes, she felt her throat tighten.

She thought back to the way they used to kiss when they were married, how unexpectedly soft and warm his lips were, how she had loved the feel of the little patch of stubble that he often missed just beneath his mouth.

'That's what you used to do when you wanted a kiss,' Sid said with a smile.

'Stop it,' she replied, a little too defensively.

'I just meant—'

'What?'

'I was trying to explain that . . . that I remember you tipping your head back and pouting like that.'

'I wasn't pouting,' she said. 'What are you talking about?'

'I said—'

'It sounds as though you're the paranoid one now, in case I—'

'Julia, please,' he said. 'I wasn't saying you wanted to be kissed, just that you looked like you used to when—'

'Good.'

Sid frowned and studied her. 'What's going on here?'

'I just want to be clear where we both stand,' she said with a shrug.

'OK.'

'Though on the other hand, getting a kiss from your ex-husband definitely isn't as weird as being stalked by your dead fiancé,' she joked.

Sid laughed, gave her a peck on the forehead and said goodnight before setting off towards Strandvägen. Julia was still smiling as she turned away from him, but all she really felt was sadness.

She opened the door, climbed the stairs to her floor and paused to catch her breath before rummaging through her bag for her key. Once she had found it, she pushed it into the lock, let herself inside and pulled the door shut behind her.

In the darkness of the hallway, she closed her eyes. Her cane clattered to the floor, and then the silence took over.

The loneliness gripping her heart was all too familiar. She had first come face to face with it when she was much too young, and she knew it would never let her go.

A slow-motion camera flash illuminated the memory of the four coffins in the church.

She saw the scene from above, a young girl sitting all alone in the front row of pews. And on the stone floor in the aisle beside her, there were two crutches.

Julia's phone started ringing in her bag, dragging her back to the present.

She kicked off her shoes, struggled out of her coat, let it drop to the floor behind her and made her way through to the kitchen before she answered.

'Hello?' said a hesitant voice. 'My name is Bianca Salo, I've been trying to reach you.'

'Yes, I read your email. I was planning to give you a call in the morning,' Julia replied as she started the voice recorder on her phone.

'I'm sorry to bother you so late, but—'

'Don't worry.'

The woman let out a sob, and it sounded as though she was walking across a creaky wooden floor, opening and closing a door. Her breathing was unsteady, and when she next spoke Julia realised she could hear a note of hysteria in her voice.

'I . . . I'm too scared to go home,' Bianca continued. 'I'm still in my dressing room at the theatre . . . My friend is here with me, but she has to go soon, and I don't know what to do.'

'Could you tell me what happened?' Julia asked as she sat down on one of the chairs at the table.

'You're the one who solved the china dolls case, aren't you?'

'Yes.'

'I remember, I read all about it. That was incredible,' said Bianca.

'Thank you.'

Another voice said something in the background, and Julia heard a clothes hanger screech against a rail.

'Do you think you . . . that you might be able to help me?' Bianca asked.

'What do you need help with?'

'This is going to sound crazy, but I'm not, I swear. You're going to think I'm getting worked up over nothing . . . Honestly, I wish I was, but this is real. I'm not mentally ill,' Bianca said, swallowing hard.

'Take your time.'

'I think I've got a stalker, and . . . I really wish I could say I was exaggerating just to pique your interest, but it's my fiancé, Nicolás.'

She trailed off, and Julia heard her whisper something.

'You mentioned in your email that he was dead,' Julia said after a moment.

'He is . . . He's dead,' Bianca replied, as though she was trying to convince herself.

'So what makes you think he's stalking you?'

'I saw him. I woke up and saw him in my bedroom last night. You can probably see why I don't want to go home . . .'

'Are you sure it wasn't just a dream?'

'I know how it sounds, but he took his cufflinks. They were in a little dish on my dresser.'

'Were you scared?'

'It probably doesn't *sound* that bad,' Bianca replied, taking a shaky breath. 'But something else happened, too . . . Before he took the cufflinks, he held a finger up to his throat . . . You know, in a kind of cutting motion.'

'And did you interpret that as a death threat?'

'Honestly, I don't even want to think about it. None of this makes any sense,' she said.

'What motive could Nicolás have to stalk you?' asked Julia.

'I don't know, but I've . . . I've moved on with my life, been seeing other people.'

'Where do you live?'

'Nytorget, but I can't go home. I can't stay here, either, because I think he's been in my dressing room as well. Someone set fire to my dress on Thursday. I smelled smoke as soon as

8

I came off stage, and I saw it when I came down here to get changed.'

'What's the name of the friend you have with you now?'

'Regina.'

'Could you stay at her place tonight?' asked Julia.

'Not tonight, that won't work.'

Julia heard the other voice in the background again.

'OK,' said Bianca. 'She says she has time to drive me home if we leave now. If I wait in the 7-Eleven across the square from my building, would you come and make sure Nicolás isn't in my apartment? Otherwise I actually have no idea what I'm going to do.'

Two

JULIA STARK USED HER CANE to steady herself as she got out of the taxi in Nytorget and turned towards the 7-Eleven. Through the fogged-up window, she saw a blonde woman with a furrowed brow sitting at one of the tables. The woman was in full view of everyone who happened to be walking by, the pale glow of her phone illuminating her face, fingers slowly swiping across the screen, a can of Coca-Cola on the table in front of her.

Julia went back over her phone call with Bianca.

The actress had woken up in the middle of the night and seen her dead fiancé in her dark bedroom. He used a finger to mime slitting his own throat, then took his cufflinks from a bowl on the dresser and left the apartment.

By getting involved in the case, Julia's primary role would be stopping the stalker before he went too far. She couldn't allow herself to get bogged down by the question of whether or not the fiancé was really dead, though she knew she would likely have to look into it in order to get to the truth.

She made her way into the 7-Eleven, across the dirty floor, and paused in front of the woman sitting by the window.

'Bianca?'

Julia saw a flicker of fear in the actress's big brown eyes before she realised who had just spoken to her.

'Thank you for coming,' she said as she got to her feet.

When Bianca noticed the scar on Julia's face, she didn't instinctively look away like most other people. Instead, she studied the long mark with interest for a moment before holding out a hand.

'I don't shake hands,' said Julia.

'OK,' said Bianca, letting her outstretched hand drop to her side without seeming the least bit surprised.

Bianca Salo had a round, symmetrical face, and there was something almost doe-like about her wide-set eyes. Her shapely lips, with their pronounced Cupid's bow, made her look like she was always smiling softly, a moment away from laughter.

She was beautiful, no doubt about it, but there was also something ordinary and dishevelled about her.

'I've never met a real-life detective before,' she said admiringly.

'Ta-da,' Julia replied with a smile.

'So what happens now?'

'We'll start by checking your apartment, and then we can sit down and talk about what I can do for you.'

'I feel calmer already,' said Bianca, taking one last swig of her Coke before leaving the can on the table.

In silence, the two women walked over to a building from the turn of the last century. It had muted yellow walls, bay windows and white woodwork. Bianca entered a code on the number pad by the entrance, and the lacquered oak door automatically swung open.

12

They got into the lift, and Julia pressed up against the back wall to avoid any unwanted physical contact.

'You can wait outside while I check the apartment,' she said.

She recognised the subtle scent of Bianca's perfume, a delicate fragrance with heart notes of iris, geranium and possibly lilac.

'I'm getting really nervous now,' said Bianca.

'Why?'

'In case he's still in there.'

'I doubt he is.'

'But imagine.'

'If he is, then this will be my quickest case to date,' Julia replied with a smile.

'Seriously, though.'

'I have some pepper spray in my bag,' she lied.

'OK.'

The creaking lift slowed and came to a halt on the fourth floor, and Bianca opened the gate. The lightbulb on the ceiling flickered anxiously inside its rounded glass shade.

'Go a little further up the stairs,' said Julia.

'My place is a bit of a mess,' the actress apologised as she rummaged through her bag.

'I'm sure I've seen worse.'

'Good,' Bianca replied with a smile, dropping a red leather key case into her hand.

'Go and wait on the stairs.'

Julia pushed the key into the lock and let herself into the apartment. From the dark hallway on the other side, warm air flooded towards her, carrying the aroma of soap and fresh flowers.

She stepped inside, turned on the light and listened carefully, leaning against her cane. Beside the overflowing shoe rack, she noticed, there was a plastic bag full of empty wine bottles. Photographs of Bianca and her friends had been pushed in beneath the frame around the edges of the mirror.

A dog barked briefly elsewhere in the building, but other than that Julia couldn't hear a thing.

She opened the coat cupboard and used her cane to push the garments aside, then made her way through to the bathroom. It was tiled from floor to ceiling, and behind the blue polka dot shower curtain there was an enamel bathtub with a rusty stain beneath the dripping tap. The vanity unit was cluttered with makeup and cleaning products, the mirror flecked with toothpaste. A pair of black knickers with a pantyliner still stuck to them had been dropped on the floor.

Julia went back out into the hallway and noted that the front door had neither a security chain nor a peephole. Bianca's voice drifted through to her from the stairwell. She seemed to be on the phone to someone, poking fun at her own hysteria.

Julia continued through a glass door into a pretty room with a rounded bay window. In one corner, a slab of pale concrete hinted at where a tiled stove had once stood to heat the room. There were books and scripts everywhere, stacked up against the walls, on the TV unit and below the overloaded bookshelf.

On the walls, Bianca had a number of framed posters from plays in which she had starred – *The Seagull*, *A Doll's House* and *Miss Julie* – and the sagging sofas and armchairs were all cluttered with cushions and blankets.

There were several bowls of old olive pits and pistachio shells, dirty coffee cups, wine glasses and mugs containing dried teabags dotted about the room, seemingly forgotten, on the coffee table, on top of the piles of books and on the piano.

Julia noticed a dog-eared pack of tarot cards on a small pedestal table. Three of the cards had been dealt out, two of them face up: the High Priestess and the Wheel of Fortune.

She checked behind the sofa and then pulled back the curtains in the bay window. Once she was satisfied there was no one there, she went through to the cramped kitchen. A large hammered copper pot had been left to dry on a checked tea towel on the counter beside the old gas hob, and on the drop-leaf table, there was a half-eaten piece of toast with some sliced cucumber on top. Beside a vase of drooping roses, she noticed a film script on top of an open envelope.

Julia's thoughts turned back to her dinner with Sid and the fact that she hadn't managed to have a frank chat with him about the future. She needed to pluck up the courage to ask whether he was interested in a trial working full-time as a private detective, possibly even becoming a partner in the firm. Her dream was that they would share an office, sitting across from each other every day, drinking coffee in the morning, discussing strategy, eating lunch together and working late into the evening.

Just last week, she had made a spur-of-the-moment decision to buy an antique desk for him, then immediately felt stupid and had it put into storage.

Julia glanced out through the doors onto the balcony, at the plants, the small white table, the wicker sofa and the yellow and orange cushions. She heard a soft clinking sound as a clothes peg on the washing line swung against the inside of the railing.

Julia was just about to turn around when something shiny caught her eye. It was black, and almost looked like polished carbon steel. It took her a moment to process what she was looking at, but then she realised what it was: a beak, the feathers around it rustling in the breeze. There was a dead crow wedged between two cushions on the sofa outside.

Three

JULIA SHOOK OFF HER UNEASE and went through to the dark bedroom. The walls were pink, and there was a Persian rug on the floor, crumpled black silk sheets on the bed. On one of the bedside tables, a pair of reading glasses had been left on top of a thick novel by Hilary Mantel, and in the half-open drawer Julia could see a nightguard in a plastic case, a tube of hand cream and some condoms in shiny blue wrappers.

On the other, there was a clock radio with a long antenna cable.

Julia checked the closet, used her cane to prod a garment bag and then walked over to the window to open the curtains. In the reddish-brown building on the other side of the narrow street, a man with silvery hair was standing in one of the windows, staring straight at her.

Julia walked back through to the front door and popped her head out into the stairwell. Bianca was waiting ten steps up, arms wrapped tightly around herself.

'There's no one here,' said Julia.

'Phew,' the actress replied with a sigh, as though she had been holding her breath.

'But there is a dead bird on your balcony.'

'I know, I saw that. It's horrible. I've been trying to psych myself up to get rid of it.'

'Shall we sit down and have a chat?' asked Julia.

Bianca came towards her and took the keys. Once they were both inside the apartment, she locked the door and tried the handle before following Julia through to the kitchen.

She moved the vase of flowers over to the counter and then sat down opposite Julia with a look of weariness on her face.

'So, what can my agency and I help you with?' Julia asked.

'I just feel so damn unsafe ... You know, it gets in here,' Bianca replied, with a gesture to her head. 'I don't have the energy to be scared all the time.'

'I understand.'

'That's the most important thing, that nothing happens. That he can't follow me and hurt me.'

'I'm not a bodyguard, but I will find and stop your stalker.'

'Do I *need* a bodyguard?' Bianca asked, fiddling with the salt shaker.

'I don't know enough to be able to answer that – I'll need to talk to my contact on the police force first – but we'll do our very best to guarantee your safety in the meantime.'

Bianca squinted at her with a slight smile. 'Are you always this confident?'

'When it comes to uncovering the truth, I am.'

'I've looked into the cost of a bodyguard,' Bianca continued. 'I don't know how much you charge, but if you can do what you say you can then I figure it'll work out cheaper in the long run.'

'Once a stalker develops a fixation, they tend to be pretty persistent,' said Julia. 'There's a famous artist who was stalked by the same person for thirty-five years.'

'Jesus,' said Bianca, letting out a deep sigh.

'This is my standard contract, with the rolling costs laid out,' Julia explained, taking out a plastic folder. 'But I can also give you a flat fee quote, if you'd prefer.'

'Which is best?'

'Rolling costs would probably be best for you, because I tend to see results pretty quickly.'

Bianca pored over the contract and asked a few questions about the timeframe and additional expenses.

'OK, I'll sign ... On one condition,' she said with a strange glimmer in her eye.

'What?'

'Sorry, but would you be willing to stay over here tonight?' Bianca whispered. 'Just one night? I'm too scared to be on my own, and I don't have anywhere else to go.'

'If you'll let me ask you a few questions this evening.'

'Deal,' Bianca said with a smile, reaching for a pen from the windowsill. She signed the contract, slipped it back into the plastic folder and pushed it across the table.

'Thank you. Now the investigation can begin,' said Julia, studying the actress's face. 'You say that your dead fiancé is stalking you.'

'Yes,' she replied, forcing back a smile.

'Is that your way of telling me that you don't think he's really dead?'

'I thought he was until I saw him.'

'How did he die?'

'I don't actually know ... It's been a little over three years, but it still hasn't really sunk in, I ... Nicolás was on a business trip to Helsinki, and he was found dead in his hotel room. By one of the cleaners, I think.'

'You don't know what happened?'

Bianca shook her head and swallowed hard.

'I never got to see him. His body was flown back to Brazil – he was originally from Brasilia – and I wasn't invited to the funeral. No one told me anything. His family acted like I didn't even exist.'

'How did that make you feel?'

'How do you think?'

'It doesn't matter what I think. I want to know how you felt,' said Julia.

A hint of redness spread across Bianca's cheeks.

'This is hard for me to talk about,' she said softly.

'Yes.'

'It didn't feel good, like they were saying I was just some bit on the side,' she continued, her voice faltering. 'I don't know. I'm ashamed for just going along with it all, not pushing back, but I was in shock. I couldn't face getting into a fight with them. I thought his family would be decent about it.'

'That's natural.'

'Jung said that loneliness isn't about not having anyone around you, but about not being able to communicate.'

There was a thud in the living room, and Bianca flinched and managed to knock over the salt shaker. She laughed at her own jumpiness, then reached for a pinch of the spilled salt and threw it back over her left shoulder.

Four

THE TWO WOMEN WENT THROUGH to the living room and saw that a pile of books had fallen from the piano stool to the floor.

'Probably just a ghost,' said Bianca, perching on the armrest of one of the armchairs.

Julia moved over to the piano and poked at the books on the floor with her cane. A postcard from Bianca's mother had fallen out of one of them, she noticed. On it, her mother had written that she was already looking forward to the next long weekend, filling the rest of the space with little hearts.

Julia took a seat on the sofa, stretched out her leg and gazed at Bianca's face for a moment before she continued her questions.

'When did you last see Nicolás?'

'The day before he died, or whatever actually happened ... We went to Helsinki together, had a nice evening, ate at the Bellevue – I don't know if you know it?'

'No.'

'I had to fly home the next morning, because I had an important thing at the theatre. He was stuck in meetings anyway – he was a diplomat – and he had to go to something at the embassy that evening. Then he was found dead in his room the next day.'

'How did you learn that he was dead?'

'His mum sent an email saying that he'd passed away in Helsinki.'

'An email?'

Bianca nodded. 'She really just wanted to tell me to pick up my things from his apartment and leave the key in the mailbox.'

There was a soft scraping sound as a pigeon landed on the sloping window ledge outside and started sliding towards the edge.

'What did you think, when you found out that he was dead?'

'I don't really know, I kept going back and forth ... Nicolás had always had trouble sleeping, so I thought maybe he'd had a bit too much to drink and took a few too many sleeping pills ... Or that maybe he'd killed himself.'

'Was he depressed?'

'No, not at all. Not as far as I know, anyway. But he was under a huge amount of pressure from his family.'

'What sort of pressure?'

The pigeon slipped off the window ledge and flapped in the air.

'To be as successful as the rest of them. He was trying so hard, and he had a pretty good career,' Bianca replied. 'Honestly, I don't want anything to do with his family. I don't know ... You assume that when something like this happens, a tragedy ... you assume that people will forget about any old conflicts and just try to do the right thing. I mean, I'm on the verge of falling apart here. Nicolás is dead, but the same games are still going on.'

Julia felt a sinking feeling in the pit of her stomach, and she became almost weightless. She felt herself rising up onto her tiptoes, and the pressure on the handle of her cane eased.

On the other side of the window, the pigeon seemed to freeze in mid-air, its wings moving so slowly that she could see the feathers hooking together to form a smooth, stable surface.

Her eardrums retracted, and an underwater roar took over.

Julia turned to Bianca and saw her eyes glisten just before they welled up.

Her lips closed, her pupils widened.

She slowly raised a hand to her mouth.

The pigeon's wings forced the air downwards, and a bluish-grey feather came loose and swirled away.

Julia followed Bianca's eyeline.

The actress had absentmindedly glanced over to a section of the bookshelf where the paperbacks had been stacked up with their spines facing outwards.

Behind them, Julia could make out a metal safe door.

Bianca blinked, and the tears started spilling down her cheeks.

Her hand was still covering her mouth.

Just before time returned to its usual speed, Julia decided that there must be something relating to Nicolás's death inside the safe.

She shuddered, and her body regained its usual weight.

Every now and again, time almost seemed to grind to a halt for her, as it had during the last few seconds before the plane crash that killed her family. Those quiet moments were part of her post-traumatic stress disorder, and they threw every detail into sharp relief, giving her a laser focus on what the people around her said and did.

'What games?' she asked, trying to keep her breathing calm.

Bianca lowered her hand and attempted to compose herself as she replied.

'Oh, I just mean the whole ... the fact that they completely turned their backs on me, that I'm not worth shit in their eyes. I didn't know what to do, I was all alone and had no idea what was going on ... None of them ever reached out to me. Not even his sister, who's a Swedish citizen. I mean, they know I shared a life with Nicolás, that we spent practically every day together for three years, but that meant nothing to them.'

'Strange.'

'I've never even seen the death certificate, or whatever it's called. I rang the hospital, but I didn't get anywhere. It's crazy.'

'Not particularly. Death certificates aren't public records,' Julia explained. 'You weren't married, and he also had diplomatic status.'

Bianca wiped the tears from her cheeks and tried to smile. 'So do you think I should just forget it?'

'I don't know,' Julia replied. 'But his death certificate isn't something you have any legal right to see.'

'OK.'

'What else did you mean, in terms of games?'

'I don't know, I don't know anything ... I don't even think he's really dead.'

'Shall we take a look at your bedroom?'

'It's a total mess,' Bianca said, getting up and hurrying through ahead of her.

'Don't worry.'

As she came into the room, Julia saw Bianca quickly close the drawer of the bedside table and bend over to pull the brown bedspread over the crumpled sheets.

'I've always been a bit messy, but not like this.'

Julia paused in the doorway, her eyes on the window. They were above the streetlamps, she noted, which likely meant that the bedroom was fairly dark at night.

'Where were you during the day yesterday?' she asked.

'I went to see a friend who'd been admitted to the Karolinska for surgery.'

'Who?'

'Ursula. She's going to be our prompter, but she has a problem with her vocal cords. And then I had a performance at seven.'

'*The Seagull?*'

'Yes,' Bianca replied with a nod.

'Did you come straight home after that?'

'Yes.'

'What time was it when you saw Nicólas?'

'Half-three in the morning.'

'OK, so you were lying in bed. Where was he?' asked Julia.

'Over by the dresser.'

'Did he notice that you'd seen him?'

'I want to say no, because he didn't say anything ... But I think he did. It felt that way, anyway. In the room, between us.'

'What do you mean?' Julia asked, moving over to the dresser.

'I can't explain it.'

'He took a pair of cufflinks out of here,' said Julia, touching a small bowl of jewellery.

'Yes ... Well, he made the cutting motion across his throat first, then he took the cufflinks, and then he left.'

'Can you show me exactly what he did? Is it OK if I lie down on your bed?'

'Sure.'

Julia propped her cane against the bedside table, took a seat on the edge of the mattress, shuffled back and lay down.

'Like this?'

'Yes,' said Bianca.

'And you saw him as soon as you woke up?'

'He was standing here,' said Bianca, moving over to the dresser and half-turning towards the bed.

'Wasn't the room dark?'

'Yes, but the display on Nicolás's clock radio is pretty bright.'

'So you could tell that he was looking at you?'

Bianca took a deep breath. 'I was just lying there, frozen ... My heart was racing. He was standing here, and then he turned away and ...'

Bianca dragged a finger across her throat, turned her back to Julia, pretended to take a pair of cufflinks out of the bowl and then left the room. A moment later, she came back.

'You weren't looking at me when you gestured to your throat,' said Julia.

'That's how he did it, and a second later he was gone.'

'Did he close the front door behind him?'

'Closed and locked it.'

'So he had a set of keys?'

'Of course.'

The locked door both strengthened and weakened Bianca's claim, thought Julia. If the whole thing was a dream, then of course the door would have been locked when she woke, but if she really had seen Nicolás in her room, then he could also have locked it behind him.

'What did you do once he had gone?'

'What did I do? I stayed in bed and ... I don't know, closed my eyes and prayed to God until I was sure he was gone. I listened for a while, then I rang Ramon, one of my colleagues, who told me to call the police. So I did that, and they got here pretty quickly, checked the apartment. What could they say, though? There was nothing for them to do. They just said that they didn't think I was likely to get the cufflinks back.'

'Did you tell them you thought it was Nicolás?'

'No,' Bianca replied with a sad smile.

'And then what?'

'Ramon came over to get me. I stayed at his for the rest of the night, but he's got his kids there now, so I couldn't stay there again today.'

Five

J ULIA WAS SITTING ON THE sofa in the living room when Bianca carried two steaming cups of tea through from the kitchen and set them down on the coffee table. She apologised again for the mess, tidying away a couple of empty glasses and plates before returning to the table, picking up a spiral-bound copy of *Macbeth*, running a hand over the cover and putting it to one side on a stack of books.

'When we spoke on the phone, you said that Nicolás had been in your dressing room at the theatre, too,' said Julia, blowing on her tea.

'Yes. And before that, last week, I saw him in the audience,' she replied, taking a seat in an armchair. 'He was in the third or fourth row, just off to the left, staring straight at me.'

'Which day?'

'Tuesday.'

'OK, go on.'

'I completely choked and then ran off stage, which is a big deal. That's the kind of thing you don't do without good reason.'

Bianca's eyes wavered, and she took a deep breath.

'And the dressing room?' asked Julia.

'Like I already told you ... that was two days later.'

'Thursday, then? What time?'

'I didn't notice any smoke when I went down there during the interval.'

'What time was that?'

'Just before nine. When I went back to my dressing room after we finished, at maybe ten past ten, I could smell it right away. Something sharp and burnt. OK, I thought, that's a bit weird, but when I went to get dressed after my shower, I saw . . .'

She showed Julia a photograph of the dress, which was quite badly burnt. One side of it was completely missing, charred scraps of fabric hanging down from the melted edges, soot on the sides and top of the wardrobe.

'Who has a key to your dressing room?'

'No one other than Stina, who I share it with. We almost never lock the door, though. We're always in too much of a rush for that. And besides, the only people backstage are the ones allowed to be there.'

'How do you know?'

'Because we all have individual security passes.'

'How many people have these passes?'

'Quite a lot,' Bianca admitted. 'I know that the theatre has 330 people on a one-year contract, plus a load of others tied to specific productions and projects and God knows what else.'

This stalker has already progressed quite far, thought Julia. Not only has he been to the theatre, he has also gained access to Bianca's dressing room and set fire to one of her dresses.

That is an incredibly aggressive act.

He may have extinguished the fire before he left, but if he left the dress in flames and it somehow burnt out on its own then he represents a clear and direct threat to both her and other people.

The fact that he broke into Bianca's apartment while she slept is likely also the final step before making physical contact.

'The person you saw in your bedroom took a pair of cufflinks. Could he have gone to your dressing room first, to look for them there?'

Bianca stared at Julia with her big, wide eyes. 'Why would I have them in my dressing room?'

'I don't know, that's why I'm asking,' Julia replied. 'Could he have been looking for something else?'

'His watch, maybe?' Bianca replied without a second's thought.

A lock of blonde hair came loose and hung over her flushed cheek as she held out her left arm.

Around her wrist, she was wearing an expensive platinum watch with a laurel wreath carved into the bezel, framing the face.

'Wow,' said Julia.

'Yeah, I know. It's a Patek Philippe.'

'How much is it worth?'

'No idea, a lot ... But I would never sell it. I can't, because then I'd have nothing of Nicolás's left,' she explained. 'The family's lawyer wrote to me saying I had to give it back, but I refused.'

'I understand.'

'I guess I might be breaking the law there ... Am I?'

'Yes, but I think you should just ignore that.'

'Queen,' Bianca replied with a grin.

Julia watched the actress shake her wrist and hold the watch to her ear.

31

'Why don't you keep it in the safe?'

'I love it, always have it on.'

'But not when you're on stage?'

'No, I leave it in my dressing room then, in the small safe there. You know ... the kind with a code lock.'

'But you don't think the person who set your dress on fire was just trying to rob you?'

'No.'

Julia held her eye. 'You want me to investigate on the assumption that Nicolás is still alive and that he waited three years before he started stalking you.'

'I'm not crazy, I swear. I really have seen him twice.'

'Do you think Nicolás would be capable of hurting you?'

'No ... Not really, no. But he did get a bit jealous sometimes, and like I said, I've been trying to move on with my life.'

'With new relationships, you mean?'

'Yes,' Bianca replied with a shrug.

Julia carefully set down her teacup. 'A stalker has what a psychologist would describe as a fixation,' she explained. 'An uncontrollable, pathological obsession with another person. Over ten per cent of all people have, at one time or another, been subject to stalking to some extent. There also seems to be a kind of unwritten rule that a stalker's tolerance level keeps rising, which means they have to go further and further to get the same kick out of it. I'm not saying this to scare you, but it isn't all that uncommon for stalking to end in rape or murder.'

'So what do we do?' Bianca asked, staring at her with an open mouth.

'You've hired me, and—'

'Yes.'

'And from now on, it's incredibly important that you do as I say. I'll send you a checklist of specific things to look out for, but I can tell you right now that you need to document anything that seems even a little bit odd. Telephone calls, emails, bouquets ... People following you, showing up unexpectedly.'

'OK,' Bianca whispered.

'You need to be careful online, too. Never post where you are or what you're doing, and don't upload any pictures that might give away your location.'

'No, of course,' said Bianca, massaging the back of her neck.

'In the morning, you're going to call a locksmith and get new locks fitted, plus a security chain and a peephole. I'll talk to my contact on the police force, but we'll likely get you some security cameras, a burglar alarm and an attack alarm, too.'

'I need wine,' said Bianca. 'What do you say? Do you fancy a glass before bed?'

She got up and gave Julia an inviting smile, laughing happily when the detective said yes.

Six

BIANCA CAME BACK FROM THE kitchen carrying two wine glasses and a bottle of Côtes du Rhône. She put everything down on the coffee table, cut the foil and pulled out the cork.

Julia started telling her about how the police typically dealt with stalkers, explaining that the bar for qualifying for personal protection was so high that it was typically already too late by the time it was approved.

'Fuck it, I don't have the energy to think about this stuff right now,' Bianca muttered as she poured the wine.

They toasted, and Bianca drained half her glass in a couple of deep gulps. She then reached for the bottle and poured herself more.

'Speaking of stalkers,' she said, 'I looked you up. You're the one who survived—'

'I don't want to talk about it.'

'OK. Sorry,' Bianca said quickly, looking anxious.

'It's fine, I just don't want to talk about it.'

'Well, it's so cool that you wound up becoming a sleuth, anyway. And I think you're so pretty, with this,' she said, trailing a finger down her cheek.

'Thanks,' Julia said curtly.

She felt stiff and awkward and couldn't think of anything else to say. Bianca had noticed, she realised, and she sipped her wine in an attempt to look more relaxed.

A siren raced by somewhere in the distance, and the neighbour's dog started barking again.

'I know you would rather not have the scar, and I know I must have sounded superficial when I said it was pretty,' Bianca said quietly.

'You were just being nice.'

The actress raised her glass and drank, then wiped her lips with the back of her hand and seemed to be debating with herself.

'I've been wondering ... You talk about this police contact of yours a lot,' she said with a wry smile, shuffling a little closer.

'He's my ex-husband,' Julia confessed, conscious that her cheeks were growing hotter. 'And I've only mentioned him twice.'

'Ex-husband, huh?' Bianca tittered.

'What?'

'I can tell from your face that he's more than that,' she said with a laugh.

Julia couldn't help but smile. 'I ... I would like us to be colleagues.'

'Then go for it!' Bianca shouted, playfully slapping her leg.

'You think?'

'Why not? Or are things difficult between you?'

'No, but ...'

'Then what's the problem?'

Julia hesitated with her glass by her lips. 'He's dating someone else, and ... I'm still in love with him.'

'Uff, that sucks,' said Bianca, puffing out her cheeks.

'Yup.'

'So what are you going to do?'

'About what?'

'Winning him back, obviously.'

'That's not going to happen.'

'Are you sure?' she asked, a note of scepticism in her voice.

'Yes,' Julia whispered with a shrug.

'Well, here's to hoping.'

'Cheers.'

They brought their glasses together, making them clink. The crisp ringing sound only faded when they drank.

'OK, tell me about Nicolás,' said Julia.

'What do you want to know? He was twelve years older than me, a Scorpio. A Brazilian diplomat. Not the cultural attaché, but something along those lines.'

'How did the two of you meet?'

'I was living in a hippy commune at the time, and I met him at a culture festival in Oslo, a kind of autumn mingle ... We got engaged in the Algarve six months later.'

'Was that a surprise, or did you know it was coming?'

'The engagement? A bit of both. I didn't know he'd bought a ring and planned the whole thing out, but we had talked about it, about just going for it.'

'Did you have a party?'

'Just for the two of us, yeah. We thought it would be more romantic that way. It would've been so complicated otherwise, with my mum here in Sweden and his family in Brazil ... He's got four brothers and a sister, too, and they're scattered all over the world.'

'Did you live together?'

'We hung out with my hippy friends in the collective at first, even though he had a huge place of his own in Östermalm. And then after about a year or so, he helped me buy this place and we started spending most of our time here, because it was cosier.'

'OK, so just to make sure I've got this straight ... The two of you were together for three years, and were planning to get married, but you never officially lived together?'

'Exactly.'

'Did he speak Swedish?'

'Fluently, yeah. He'd studied here, at the School of Economics. His family has ties to Sweden too, some vague connection to the royals, they're on the boards of various Swedish companies ... I don't really know the specifics.'

Bianca yawned, poured the last of the wine into their glasses and lowered the empty bottle to the floor by her chair.

'How were things between you? Would you say you had a good relationship?'

'Yeah, for the most part.'

'Was he in love with you?'

'Yes.' Bianca smiled.

'Did he think of you as a lover? As someone to have a bit of fun with before settling down?'

'Maybe,' she replied after a moment or two, a look of sadness on her face.

'And what about the engagement?'

'I don't know, a grand gesture ... His way of getting me to stick around, because he really was in love.'

'Which one of you was most in love? Him or you?' Julia asked, intentionally trying to be provocative.

Bianca ran a hand through her hair as she thought. 'I'd say him,' she said.

'Yet you accepted his family's behaviour.'

'He hated his family!'

'Do you really believe that?'

The actress frowned.

'You think it was all just an act to keep his two worlds separate?'

'What do you think?'

'God ... you've really confused me now,' Bianca said with a sigh.

'I'm just trying to understand what your relationship was like when he died – or when his death was staged.'

'It was OK, but not always straightforward,' Bianca replied, yawning again.

'What do you mean by not always straightforward?'

'Things never are when I'm involved.'

Out of caution, Bianca held her hands above the coffee table as she took off the watch, put it down on a book and got to her feet.

'You don't keep it in the safe overnight?' asked Julia.

'Maybe I should. It honestly never occurred to me.'

She cleared away their glasses and fetched a clean towel, a new toothbrush and a pair of silvery silk pyjamas that smelled like laundry detergent. She then showed Julia where she kept her cotton pads, cleansers and night cream.

As Julia got ready for bed, Bianca made up the sofa with fresh cotton sheets, a duvet and two pillows, closed the curtains and left a large glass of cold water on the table.

'Thank you for everything,' she said as she turned off the ceiling light. 'Good night.'

'Sweet dreams,'Julia replied, plugging her phone in to charge.

She lay in the darkness, listening to Bianca pottering about in the bathroom and her bedroom until the apartment grew quiet.

Julia closed her eyes and thought about her evening. Her long dinner with Sid had ended badly because, as ever, she had wanted too much from him. Just half an hour after his peck on the forehead outside her building, she had come over to her new client's apartment, had a few glasses of wine and was now – in a slightly unorthodox turn of events – sleeping over on her sofa.

Chatting to Bianca had been interesting, and the actress had clearly started to question her position in Nicolás's life over the course of their conversation. They weren't married and didn't live together, which meant that neither the marriage nor cohabitation acts applied to them.

Legally speaking, there was nothing tying them together.

Nothing but love and attraction.

Julia felt her face grow hot again as she remembered she had allowed Bianca to coax her into talking about Sid, about her unrequited love and her plan to make him a partner.

She rolled over on the sofa, gazing out across the dark room, at the stacks of books by the walls.

From the street down below, she could hear the muffled sound of voices.

Julia thought there was something shaky about Bianca's account of her stalker, like a glass of water on a high-speed train.

So far, there had been three incidents.

Bianca could easily have been mistaken in the theatre, dazzled by the bright lights. But even if that was the case, the fact that she *thought* she had seen her dead fiancé in the audience may well have caused her to dream about him.

Dreaming about waking up is an incredibly common form of parasomnia.

Nicolás's visit to her bedroom felt real to Bianca, which meant it became a matter of fact alongside the shock of seeing him in the theatre. And as a result, she had naturally connected both to the incident in her dressing room.

Perhaps the theft of the cufflinks from her apartment was simply a lie of necessity, something Bianca had thought up because she realised she wouldn't sound credible otherwise.

Perhaps she didn't have a stalker at all, Julia thought drowsily. The burnt dress was the only concrete piece of evidence they had, after all.

Her eyes drifted over to the strange floor lamp, which had a glass cover over its metal frame and a round shade featuring large prisms.

Julia felt her eyelids growing increasingly heavy, and as she drifted towards sleep she tried to remember what she had noticed when time ground to a halt earlier.

She closed her eyes.

Her dark field of vision flickered, and she saw floating flames, droplets of mercury, bare trees with sprawling branches.

Julia could smell old books, and she pictured the packed bookcase. With that, she suddenly remembered what it was.

When she spoke about Nicolás's death, Bianca's eye had been subconsciously drawn to the safe. There was a clue to whatever happened in Helsinki locked behind that solid metal door.

Seven

J
ULIA WAS ALREADY DRESSED AND ready when Bianca's
radio alarm clock went off at five to seven. The two women
said good morning, poured themselves a couple of cups of
strong coffee and sat down in the kitchen.

'You should call a locksmith right away,' Julia reminded her,
leaning her cane against the little table.

'I don't know what to ask for.'

'Do you have a pen and paper?'

Bianca reached for a pen from the windowsill and put it
down on top of a film script. On the back, Julia wrote the name
of two different types of door guard, a high-quality peephole
and the kind of lock she should ask for.

The actress then called a local locksmith and managed to
charm him into prioritising her and coming straight over.

The warm morning sun was spilling in through the window,
shining dully on the ergonomic handle of Julia's cane. It had
been custom-made for her by the rehabilitation unit, using a
cast of her hand in order to provide maximum relief.

Bianca flitted around the room in her pink kimono, taking
out yoghurt and muesli, bowls and spoons, a wooden chopping
board and a small knife.

'Try some pomegranate in your muesli,' she said, setting down a basket of passion fruit, kiwis, pomegranates and grapes on the table.

'The problem is I can never say no to passion fruit,' Julia told her. 'It's a kind of everyday magic, you know? Because I never want to say no to passion in my life.'

'Does that work?' asked Bianca.

'A woman can always hope,' she replied with a smile, slicing the fruit in two.

As they ate, Julia decided that she should start trying to map out Bianca's personal contacts. The actress might have been convinced that it was Nicolás who was stalking her, but Julia had to make sure she kept an open mind.

More often than not, a stalker had some sort of concrete connection to their victim.

If Bianca's stalker wasn't an employee of the theatre, then perhaps they were one of the other actors' girlfriends, someone's boyfriend or ex.

'Who might have been near your dressing room on Thursday?' Julia asked as she started tucking into the tangy fruit with a teaspoon.

'Basically everyone at the theatre,' Bianca replied with a shrug.

'I need to try to find out if anyone saw anything,' Julia explained, crunching on the little black seeds.

'OK, well, the whole cast of *The Seagull* was there … and there was also a voluntary workshop for everyone involved in *Macbeth.*'

'Quite a few people, in other words.'

'I need to go and get ready,' Bianca said, hurrying through to her bedroom to get dressed.

Julia reached for her cane, got up and rinsed out the two coffee cups and bowls.

The buzzer rang, and she went out into the hallway to answer. A man with a full ginger beard and tattooed arms held out a parcel. He was wearing a T-shirt with a large key on the front.

'This was by the door,' said the locksmith.

'Thanks.'

He pushed his trolley of equipment into the hall, and Julia carried the parcel back through to the kitchen and set it down on the table. It was a small box tied with brown string, the address written by hand. Bianca came into the kitchen in nothing but her underwear, poured herself a glass of water and took a sip to wash down a pill.

'Do you know what this is?' Julia asked her.

'Looks like it's from Sonny, my ex,' she replied.

'Can I open it?'

'Yeah, if you want.'

Julia put on a pair of latex gloves and sliced open one side of the box. She then pulled out a wad of wood wool and found a glass jar containing something red.

'Raspberry jam,' said Bianca.

The jar had a glass lid, the kind that could only be removed by pulling on a green rubber tab to break the seal. On the label, in neat blue letters, someone had written:

Wool of bat and tongue of dog, adder's fork and blindworm's sting.

'It doesn't say raspberry jam,' said Julia.

'That's a quote from *Macbeth*.'

'Does your ex often send you jam?'

'No, but I do get letters from time to time.'

'What does he write?'

'That I'm always welcome to come home,' Bianca replied, holding Julia's gaze with her big brown eyes.

'Has he been having trouble letting you go?'

'Sonny? Oh, no, he's not a stalker,' she said with a smile.

'What's his surname?'

'Grünewald.'

'How can you be so sure he isn't stalking you?' asked Julia.

'Because Sonny is more interested in himself than anything.'

'But he sends you jam.'

'Yeah, but that's only because he thinks it'll make me think about him and long to return to paradise,' she replied. 'He lives out in the sticks. A bit alternative, I guess you could say.'

Julia sat down at the computer in her office on Styrmansgatan and created an Excel spreadsheet to map out everything she knew so far.

Back at Bianca's apartment, she had made the locksmith a cup of coffee and then returned to the kitchen and put the jam jar into an evidence bag.

Once the new locks had been fitted, Bianca came out into the hall wearing a yellow dress and a pair of large gold hoops in her ears. With a dazzling smile, she had thanked the locksmith for his help, and he had smiled shyly, packed up his things and left.

Bianca gave Julia a spare set of keys and, with a laugh, explained that she hadn't just dressed up for the locksmith. It was the final performance of *The Seagull* that evening, and she and the rest of the cast were going out to celebrate afterwards.

Julia had walked over to Skanstull metro station, felt a rush of anxiety on the escalator down to the platform and pulled on her thin leather gloves. The middle carriages in the first northbound train were a bit too busy for her liking, so she decided to wait.

Three trains passed before she finally saw one that felt suitably empty.

At every station, there were ads for a new Netflix series featuring huge pictures of Bianca with a provocative look in her eyes and sopping wet hair.

Julia desperately wanted to call Sid to tell him about the case, to try to pique his interest and possibly even ask him for a first favour – such as talking to the victim and personal safety unit, knocking on doors in Bianca's building or sending the jam off for analysis.

She sat with the phone in her hand for a while, then put it back down on the desk. She didn't quite feel brave enough to talk to him yet, not after the stupid misunderstanding about kisses last night.

Julia labelled Bianca's keys with her client number, then hung them on one of the hooks in her filing cabinet. She returned to her desk, made a note of everything she had done so far, got back up and wandered through to the pantry to see if she had anything nice to eat. There was a single biscuit left at the bottom of a tube, and she took it back to her desk, prised off the delicate top half and ate the various components in turn: first the vanilla cream, then the jam and last of all, the biscuit itself.

Who are you, Bianca? she asked herself. *Through which window are you being watched?*

Using a ghost account, Julia started following Bianca on Instagram and scrolled through row after row of glamorous photographs from fashion shoots and premieres, pausing on a picture from the Guldbagge Awards.

Among all the tuxedos and shimmering gowns, Bianca stood out. Her nose was sunburnt, and she was casually dressed in a pair of tight leather trousers and a T-shirt with the words 'What the fuck is f**k?' printed across the chest.

Just off to one side, a man with a blurry face was staring at her.

Everything Bianca does is public, Julia thought. There are so many eyes on her, all of the time.

She started working her way through every post and comment since Bianca's first upload nine years ago, singling out any followers whose comments seemed either strange or too involved and enthusiastic.

She didn't find any explicit threats, but since Bianca was fairly active on there, constantly showering her followers with hearts, it seemed likely that she deleted any sexist or negative comments.

A follower with the username *bonita66* seemed particularly fixated on Bianca's clothing and appearance. Another, *emil-peterson*, frequently asked oddly critical questions.

A number of users seemed to think of themselves as Bianca's real friends, and countless others labelled themselves her greatest admirers.

All these followers are stalkers to some extent, Julia thought as she started searching the news archive for any articles or interviews with Bianca, gradually piecing together an overview of her life.

Bianca was the only child of Anna Salo and Maxim Hammar, both of whom had worked in advertising. Her parents separated when she was nine, and she had split her time between Stockholm and Saltsjöbaden until she was accepted onto the theatre programme at Södra Latin school. Her teacher there was a man called Antonio Alonso, and according to various interviews she had given over the years, he was the one who had really sparked her passion for acting.

Bianca had won a place at drama school in Stockholm when she was nineteen, and put on a production of *Medea* as her final performance. The autumn after graduating, she managed to get a small part in Henrik Ibsen's *The Wild Duck* at the Royal Dramatic Theatre. She was in a relationship with Sonny at that point, and spent as much time with him as she could. Over the next few years, she was cast in a handful of other minor roles, and also made a cameo in a Swedish crime series on TV.

Bianca then met Nicolás Castelo, got engaged to him in Portugal and, at the age of just twenty-eight, bagged the first major part of her career, as Lady Macbeth – again at Dramaten. The production was roundly panned, with the critics almost unanimous in describing it as a fiasco. Bianca bore the brunt of the blame, amid accusations that she lacked depth and was too young for the part. Less than two weeks after the premiere, she had a breakdown mid-show, and the rest of the run was cancelled.

Ironically, it was only after that traumatic experience that Bianca Salo's career really took off. She got a permanent job at Dramaten, and one juicy part followed another.

Now, three years later, the theatre was putting on a new production of Shakespeare's most famous tragedy, and Bianca had yet again been cast as Lady Macbeth.

The artistic director seemed to want to atone for the past by giving everyone a second chance, with Regina Muhammed back in the director's role and Mikko Järvinen playing Macbeth.

Now, a few days after the news broke, Bianca had received a jar of jam from Sonny Grünewald.

Julia drummed her nails on the desk and asked herself whether there was some sort of hidden aggression in sending a jar of jam labelled with the ingredients of a witches' brew.

Eight

J ULIA STARK WAS HEADING NORTH on the motorway in the backseat of a black car, debating whether or not to put together a comprehensive suspect profile.

As a rule, stalkers can generally be divided into two groups: psychotic and non-psychotic. Bianca's stalker seemed structured, which meant that he or she likely belonged to the latter.

Among the non-psychotic group, narcissistic and antisocial personality disorders were not uncommon.

The driver sped up once they passed Åkersberga, on a road that meandered through forests and past fields.

Julia's thoughts drifted, yet again, to the fact that Bianca's ex had written *Wool of bat and tongue of dog, adder's fork and blindworm's sting* on the label of the jam jar he had sent her. It was a quote from the play Bianca was due to start rehearsing soon, and was likely meant as a joke, but at the same time it seemed clear that he hadn't accepted that their relationship was over.

They turned off into the small community of Wira Bruk, which, during Sweden's period as a great power, had been home to the most important ironworks in the country.

Through the dust thrown up from the gravel track, Julia could see the red wooden buildings, the bridges over the stream and the waterlilies on the pond.

The road snaked on, through clusters of trees and across meadows.

Sonny Grünwald had neither a phone number nor a social media presence, he didn't own a vehicle and had never married, but he had been registered as living in the same location for years.

Julia knew that, statistically, men from previous relationships are the most dangerous kind of stalker.

The car reached the top of a hill, and the landscape opened out in front of them.

Between the glittering dikes, there were a number of well-tended fields surrounded by weather-beaten fences.

The satnav had just announced that they would reach their destination in two hundred metres when the houses came into view behind a small copse.

They pulled in between the gates and came to a halt. Julia gripped her cane, asked the driver to leave the meter running, and got out of the car.

The sunshine was blinding, the air heavy with the scent of greenery, insects buzzing around the sunflowers and poppies.

She started walking towards the cluster of red wooden houses with mossy roofs.

With its well and hand pump, irrigation system, large reservoirs and simple wind turbine, barns, sheds, woodpiles, beehives, fruit trees and woven baskets of apples, the farm looked idyllic.

She saw the sun flash on a row of greenhouses a little further back.

A heavily pregnant woman, near-naked, was sitting on a bench in the shade of the main house, whittling a bowl. She had a shaved head, and her bare face was pretty yet stern. Her breasts were large, her nipples dark, and she had veiny arms and stretchmarks on her taut belly.

'Is Sonny here?' Julia called over to her.

The woman glanced across to a man with a bare chest who was standing beside an outdoor kitchen a little further away. His sun-bleached hair was plaited, and he was wearing nothing but a sarong, a greyish-brown scrap of material tied around his hips.

Julia walked over to him and was greeted by the wonderful aroma of toasted spices. Fennel seed, curry leaves, cardamom, cumin and coriander.

The man seemed to be brimming with energy, and he tapped his wooden spoon on the edge of his large cast-iron pot and turned to Julia.

His face was clean-shaven, and he had laughter lines and a gap between his front teeth.

'That smells incredible,' Julia told him, leaning against her cane.

'Beans, carrots, lentils, tomatoes ... All grown here,' he said. 'Aside from the coconuts, obviously. For the coconut oil. I bartered with a friend in the Philippines for those.'

'What did they get in return?'

'Money.'

'Ha,' said Julia.

Another woman, this one wearing jeans and a sweaty vest, walked past the yard pushing a wheelbarrow full of muddy potatoes.

'Stay and break bread with us,' said Sonny.

'Thank you, but—'

'You didn't wind up here by chance.'

'No.'

'So maybe you should stop flirting and ask what she wants,' the pregnant woman muttered, blowing the wood shavings from her bowl.

'I'm here to ask you to give back Bianca's key,' Julia explained.

'What key?'

'To her apartment.'

'She told you I have a key to her apartment?' Sonny asked, squinting at Julia.

'No ... it was a long shot on my part.'

'Would you mind telling me who you are?'

'Julia Stark, private detective.'

'And you came out here to ask if I've got a key belonging to—'

'Bianca has a stalker.' Julia cut him off.

'I'm sorry to hear that.'

'Yet you don't seem surprised.'

'Are you?'

Butterflies flitted over the wildflowers nearby.

'Why did you send jam to Bianca?'

Julia instinctively backed away when he took a step towards her, and she caught a flash of disappointment in his eyes before he replied.

'So she'll remember paradise when she dives headlong into Shakespeare's darkness and gets blood all over her hands,' he said, holding her gaze.

'Did you go to her apartment?'

'I haven't been anywhere. Everything I want comes to me here,' he said with a smile.

'You quoted the ingredients of a witches' brew on the label.'

'Was that wrong? Maybe it was. I thought it sounded good.'

The second woman reappeared around the corner of the house carrying a broom and started brushing the wooden slats beneath an outdoor shower. On a large tripod made from stripped tree trunks, there was a tank of sun-warmed water.

'It's a beautiful place you've got here,' said Julia.

'Thanks. We're almost self-sufficient, and we get some EU subsidies,' he said. 'But if needs be, we check between the sofa cushions for any money gathering dust there ... Either that or we sell natural medicines.'

'Maybe it's time the pig went on her way,' said the pregnant woman.

'She's not a pig,' Sonny replied.

'... Before she finds out what kind of medicine you're growing in the greenhouses,' she continued.

'I'm not interested in any of that,' Julia reassured them.

Sonny stirred the pot, used a small spoon to taste the stew, then added a little lemon zest and stirred it again.

'You and Bianca were together seven years ago,' said Julia.

'Yes, she lived here,' he replied, tapping the wooden spoon on the edge of the pot.

'Why did you break up?' Julia asked, taking a seat on a stool.

'She met Nicolás.'

'How did that make you feel?'

'Good.'

'Good?'

'I liked him, it was all cool. He and Bianca used to chill here when they weren't working, for ... it must've been at least a year, I'd say.'

'While they were together?'

'Young and wild and free.'

'Maybe I'm just old-fashioned, but that doesn't exactly square with my idea of a diplomat's life.'

'It was high summer, and everything was lush and green when the snake arrived in the form of a black limousine. It drove right up here, across the grass, to collect Nicolás,' Sonny explained. 'He took one last drag on my joint, kissed Bianca on the lips and then set off for Brazil. To see some people from the foreign office, I think. Their foreign office ... And then he started working at the embassy on Kungsgatan and suddenly wanted to cut and comb his hair, wear a tie and proper shoes. Bianca stopped coming over here, and we lost touch.'

'What did you make of that?'

'Of what?'

'Of Bianca choosing a different path.'

'She wanted to be a star. That's not going to happen if you live in paradise.'

'Hmm,' said Julia.

With a sigh, the pregnant woman got up and brushed the wood shavings from her belly. The elastic in her yellow knickers was on its last legs.

'Use a condom if you sleep with him,' she said over her shoulder as she waddled into the house.

'What did you make of Nicolás's choice? Becoming a diplomat?' Julia continued.

'He came from a rich family, and rich families have a real gravitational pull ... Sooner or later, they always haul the kids back in, regardless of how free they might think they are,' Sonny replied. 'His sister's probably the only one who actually did her own thing. She's a UN peacekeeper in South Sudan. And I think there's a brother who was a pretty famous DJ before he became the education secretary in the last Brazilian government.'

'What did you think when you heard that Nicolás was dead?'

For the first time during their conversation, Sonny seemed completely taken aback. 'What did you just say?' he stuttered. 'Nicolás is dead? No, I can't believe it.'

'Why not?'

'It just doesn't feel like he is.'

Sonny's fair brows were knitted, and he nodded his head slowly as though he was trying to process the news.

'You hadn't heard that he'd died?' asked Julia.

'This is terrible ... Man, how is Bianca? I mean ...'

'She's doing OK,' said Julia.

'Yeah.'

'It was three years ago.'

'Seriously?'

'Do you have any idea who could be stalking Bianca?'

'No, but ...'

He trailed off and crushed some flaked salt in his hand.

'What were you going to say?'

'Just that there's always a kind of electricity in the air between the people around Bianca ... They're always competing to stay close to her,' he replied, sprinkling the salt into his stew.

'Are you thinking of anyone in particular?'

'I haven't seen her in years, so I couldn't say who they are right now, but I have no doubt she has people interested in her.'

'If you think of anything else, I'd really appreciate it if you would let me know,' Julia said, getting to her feet and handing Sonny her card.

'I often say that leaving paradise is the most human quality.'

Julia walked down the slope, got back into the air-conditioned car and saw that the other woman was now in the shower, holding her joint clear of the water in her outstretched hand.

After they passed through Wira Bruk and pulled back out onto the main road, Julia took out her phone and called Bianca. She was going to have to take a closer look at the security system at the theatre.

Nine

JULIA SPOTTED BIANCA STANDING BY the staff entrance
on Nybrogatan, but before she had time to reach her, the
actress was accosted by a group of teenage girls desperate
to take selfies with her.

A moment later, the giggling young women thanked her and
hurried away.

Still smiling, Bianca showed Julia through to an elegant
reception area full of stone flooring, polished brass, marble and
glass.

Julia tried to explain that by agreeing to the photos with
the teenagers, Bianca had told her stalker exactly where she
was.

'God, sorry ... I didn't think,' she replied, looking troubled.

'It's OK, I just wanted to remind you to be careful. I mean,
it's hardly a secret that you might be here,' Julia said as she
walked over to the desk.

She signed in, glanced up at the security camera on the wall
above the receptionist and was given a self-adhesive visitor's
badge, which she shoved into her pocket.

Bianca was waiting off to one side, holding what looked like
some sort of hybrid between a modern electronic fob and a

traditional key. She asked if Julia was OK to take the stairs to the artistic director's office.

'That's fine.'

They went through a door with a code lock and came out into a spiral stairwell with small round windows out onto the street.

'I spoke to Wille De Geer,' Bianca said as they made their way up.

'Is that the artistic director?'

'Yeah. I love him – he's like a sweet little boy at a boarding school. Anyway, he asked if Rosmarie Björk could join us. She's the head of security, or something.'

'Great.'

The ceiling lights gleamed on the red vinyl floor.

Wille De Geer's office was at the far end of the corridor, and in the corner by the door, there was a cluster of mid-century Danish armchairs on a muted green rug.

Bianca walked straight up to the door, knocked and opened it without waiting for a reply. Julia hesitated in the doorway, leaning against her cane with both hands and watching as the actress shook hands with a woman with short grey hair before kissing the artistic director on the cheek.

'This is Julia Stark,' Bianca said. 'She doesn't shake hands.'

'Please, take a seat,' the director told Julia, gesturing to the seating area.

'On the casting couch,' Bianca added with a laugh.

Rosmarie Björk closed the door behind them, then sat down in the armchair beside the director.

A blushing Bianca explained that she had hired Stark Detective Agency – despite the fact that they clearly already knew – and then handed over to Julia.

The artistic director and the head of security studied her with serious faces.

Without mentioning Nicolás, Julia said that everything they knew so far suggested that Bianca's stalker had access to the theatre. Rosmarie Björk replied that they were aware of the incident with Bianca's dress, and that they were taking it extremely seriously.

'You have an iLOQ system,' Julia began, 'which means you should be able to check who is in the building and which doors they have accessed – and when.'

'Yes, and the system also controls which doors they're actually *able* to open,' said Rosmarie.

'We've already looked into it.' Wille spoke up, leaning back in his seat. 'But there's no sign of a break-in or any reports of unauthorised access. The only people in the building that evening – when the dress was found burnt, I mean – had a clear professional reason to be here.'

'And in the corridor by Bianca's dressing room?'

'Same . . . though fewer people,' he replied.

'Could I have their names?'

'Of course. Rosmarie will get you a list.'

Bianca took out her key and explained that while it fit the lock on her private dressing room, the electronic fob also gave her access to the rest of the theatre.

'I noticed a security camera in reception,' said Julia. 'Are there any others?'

'Ten in total, which isn't many considering the size of the building.'

'I'm assuming they cover all the unmanned entrances?'

'Correct,' said Rosmarie. 'And we've checked. No one entered the building that way on Thursday.'

'Could someone have snuck in behind a person with legitimate access?'

'That's obviously a possibility, yes ... though the idea is that all visitors are supposed to sign in.'

'How does the alarm work?'

'Securitas arms it manually every evening, to allow us more flexibility, but the system turns off automatically in the morning.'

The brief meeting came to an end with an offer to give Julia access to the theatre building. She would be provided with her own fob, the head of security explained, and the ability to access the system logs.

Both Wille De Geer and Rosmarie Björk gave her their business cards, and a promise to help in any way they could.

'Thank you,' said Julia.

Bianca was effusive, hugging them both and laughing loudly before she and Julia left the office and walked back down the corridor to the staff canteen.

The majority of people seemed to love Bianca's radiance, Julia thought, and some likely envied it. But someone had also become dangerously fixated on her.

Ten

THE STAFF CANTEEN WAS BRIGHT and spacious, with a patterned tile floor and large windows offering views across the city rooftops. There were some twenty or so people inside, sitting at the tables or standing by the food counter.

Julia's phone pinged.

Rosmarie Björk had sent her a message listing everyone who had accessed the corridor by Bianca's dressing room on Thursday. The names included the prompter and director and the whole cast of *Macbeth* other than Ramon Breiner. Five actors from *The Seagull* and a further five individuals had also been in the vicinity.

Assuming none of them were responsible for setting her dress alight, one of them must have let the person who was into the building – whether intentionally or not, manipulated into it or involved in some other way.

Someone at the theatre had to be in on it, and someone must have seen something.

Julia asked herself how long a person without access to the building could realistically manage to stay hidden inside, given all the locked areas, alarmed doors and numerous members of staff.

Overnight, perhaps, but no longer.

She heard the clatter of dishes in the kitchen.

Bianca stopped to hug a man with thinning white hair and yellow tinted lenses.

They then made their way over to the counter to buy two coffees, passing a sign announcing that the dish of the day was pork loin.

A man in leather trousers and a pink shirt was busy handing out flyers, and Bianca waved to a woman with plaited grey hair who was eating at one of the tables.

'Bianca,' the woman said with a smile as they walked over to her.

She had the sort of face that radiated joy, but her eyes were tinged with sadness. The stack of bracelets around her wrist clinked softly as she reached out to squeeze Bianca's arm.

'Do you mind if we join you?'

'At your own risk,' she replied with a smile. 'I need to wolf this soup down. I'm supposed to be down in costume at half one.'

'Me too,' said Bianca, taking a seat on a shabby chair.

'Right, I knew that.'

'This is Regina Muhammad,' Bianca told Julia. 'My best friend, visionary director and—'

'Can a woman have that title?' Regina interjected.

'And the hero who drove me home yesterday,' she rounded off.

'I'd do anything for you,' said Regina, an unexpected solemnity to her voice.

'And this is Julia Stark, of course,' Bianca continued.

'The woman who doesn't shake hands,' Regina mumbled as she continued to eat her soup.

'I'm working on that with a psychologist,' Julia said, pulling out a chair.

She steadied herself with one hand on the table, then sat down with a sigh and stretched out her leg.

'It's through our wounds that the light gets in,' said Regina. 'Nice sentiment.'

'Your colouring, it's very pretty,' Regina went on, using her sandwich to point at Julia.

'Thanks. That's ... very kind of you.'

'What about my colouring? Isn't it pretty too?' Bianca joked.

'Nope,' the director said with a smile, pinching her cheek.

'When did you first meet Bianca?' asked Julia. 'Do you remember?'

'She had a small part in a play I was directing, but she came along to every single rehearsal and often sat beside me or the prompter.'

'I just loved being here.' Bianca spoke up. 'I wanted to learn as much as I could, didn't want to miss a second.'

'We were actually rehearsing the same tragedy we'll be starting tomorrow.'

'No one dares say *Macbeth* round here,' Bianca said, smiling briefly before clapping a hand to her mouth. 'Whoops.'

'It's bad luck,' Regina explained.

'You don't believe that, though, do you?' asked Julia, holding Bianca's eye.

'Well, I was careful not to say it last time and everything still went to shit,' she replied.

'What the hell's wrong with you?' muttered an older man at one of the tables nearby.

'Who's that?' Julia asked, keeping her voice low.

'A drunk who fell off the wagon because he felt like he'd been overlooked for—'

'Hussy,' he snarled without looking at her.

'OK, ding, ding, that's the end of that round,' said Regina, turning back to her lunch.

Julia looked around the canteen, taking in as much as she could. She heard a microwave ping. Someone laughing hysterically. A bearded actor turned away and pushed a used pouch of snus tobacco into the little compartment in the lid.

Over by the counter, Julia noticed a middle-aged woman she recognised from TV. Speaking in a clear, articulate voice, she was telling a younger man about her nerves ahead of the premiere.

'I'm shitting bricks,' she said.

Regina dipped her spoon into the soup and studied Julia with a slight smile.

A man with a full face of makeup and bright red lips set down a cup of coffee on a table beside a pair of yellowed underarm shields.

'The glamorous world of theatre,' said Regina.

'I spent years working in the district court, and I can confidently say that this feels far more reasonable in every way,' Julia replied.

'Perfect,' the director said with a smile.

Over the speaker system, a voice announced that rehearsals would continue on the small stage in ten minutes.

Chair legs scraped against the floor as a group of people at one of the tables got up and shuffled out of the room.

'I'm going to need to speak to everyone involved in the production,' said Julia. 'It's routine, a bit like knocking on doors.

I just need to ask if anyone saw anything out of the ordinary. You know, someone somewhere they shouldn't have been, that sort of thing.'

'I can't even remember what I had for dinner yesterday,' Regina replied.

'No, I know, I know ... It's the same for everyone. That's why I'll need to spend a little more time chatting to you and the actors.'

'Is it OK if Julia sits in on a couple of rehearsals?' asked Bianca.

'That's fine by me, but we should probably check with everyone else. I mean, I think it'll be OK, and you can definitely come along to the first read tomorrow, to meet everyone,' Regina told Julia.

'Thank you, I'd love to.'

A man with a cup of filter coffee and a plastic-wrapped sandwich paused by their table.

'Tommy!' Bianca shouted, leaping up.

'Here, take my seat,' Regina muttered before getting up and walking away.

'Tommy is playing Duncan,' Bianca explained.

'Doomed to be murdered over and over again,' he said in a deep, rich voice.

'Unburden yourself to Julia, and I'll see you tomorrow ... both of you,' Bianca shouted as she hurried off after the director.

Eleven

TOMMY ROOS TOOK A SEAT and tore open the thin plastic wrapper around his sandwich. He then lifted off the top slice of bread, removed the lettuce and cheese, reached for a napkin and wiped away most of the thick layer of butter before putting it back together again.

'Are you a journalist?'

'Private detective,' Julia told him, pulling her hands back from the table. 'I'm helping Bianca. She has a stalker.'

He raised an eyebrow. 'Really?'

'Seems that way.'

'Wow.'

He took a big bite of his sandwich and used a hand to cover his mouth as he chewed.

Julia asked whether he had seen anyone he didn't recognise hanging around the dressing rooms recently, but he shook his head.

'Were you involved in the last production of the ... Scottish Play?'

'Yeah, everyone is back in the same roles.'

'Ah, I didn't realise that,' said Julia. 'Interesting ... But Regina just told me that Bianca only had a small part last time?'

'She did, to begin with, and she was incredible. Caught my eye straight away. She was so hungry, taking everything in . . . She learnt every part by heart and ended up stepping in as Lady Macbeth after the original actress had an accident, which was obviously doomed to fail,' Tommy explained, hesitating with his sandwich in his hand before he went on. 'But, you know, there are some mistakes you just have to make. She was young and ambitious and really wanted to give it a go. Of course she did . . . so Regina said OK, let's do it. I don't know, I felt so bad for Bianca. She'd pinned all her hopes on it, but the critics were brutal and the audiences stayed away, and . . . well, they cancelled the rest of the run after less than two weeks. There was nothing else they could do.'

'But was Bianca actually bad?' Julia asked hesitantly.

'Honestly, no,' he said, lowering his sandwich to the plate. 'Like I say, I thought she had that special something.'

'So what happened?'

'She didn't get a fair run at it. We had less than a week to rehearse, and it's not enough just to know the lines . . . I don't know, the whole thing was pretty chaotic. On a personal level, too. I mean, Bianca's fiancé punched Mikko and got thrown out of a bar, and then a few days later he was dead.'

Tommy trailed off, took a deep breath and rubbed his mouth with the back of his hand.

'What do you know about his death?' Julia asked.

'Nothing, I just heard that he died alone in a hotel room in Helsinki,' he replied, glancing down at his watch. 'Bianca was working around the clock to really inhabit the part when she heard the news, so it's really not surprising that she fell apart.'

'Do you know why Nicolás punched Mikko?' asked Julia.

'I wasn't there, but I heard it was pretty bad ... Nicolás got himself barred from Riche,' Tommy said as he got up from the table.

After her conversation with Tommy Roos, Julia Stark decided to head back to her office. A French man accosted her as she was passing the Royal Stables, announcing that she was a Norse goddess and that he wanted to marry her before asking if she knew the way to the Abba Museum.

She continued along Riddargatan, thinking about the fight at Riche and Sonny Grünewald's words about men swarming around Bianca, vying for her attention.

Once she got to her office, she sat down in an armchair and opened Bianca's Instagram feed again. Bianca had uploaded a picture of herself alone on the main stage at Dramaten thirty minutes ago, with a long caption about her sadness at having to say goodbye to the character of Nina in *The Seagull*, one of the best parts an actress could ever hope to play.

The post had already been liked by over fifteen thousand people, and there were some six hundred comments. Julia started skimming through them, but she stopped after just ten, heart racing:

Nicolas_Castelo: I've waited so long for your last performance.

Julia quickly brought up her contacts list, pressed her finger to the small picture of Sid's face and listened as the phone rang.

'Hi, this is Sidney,' he answered.

'I'm sorry to call you at work.'

'Don't worry,' he said. 'What's up?'

'Do you remember me telling you about Bianca Salo? Well, I'm now working for her, and it seems as though she has a stalker going through a particularly intense phase ... I think he might pose a genuine threat.'

There was a brief silence on the other end of the line.

'Has she been in touch with the police?'

'Yes, she has, but ... I can't say I'm all that impressed with your work protecting vulnerable women.'

'She said she thought she was being stalked by her ex-fiancé, right?' he asked in a neutral tone of voice.

'It sounds crazy, I know, but there do seem to be a lot of unanswered questions surrounding his death. I'm not saying it's him, too much time has passed, but whoever it is has a key to her flat and also managed to bypass the security system at Dramaten.'

'Oof,' said Sid.

'Yeah ... And now – and this is why I'm ringing – the stalker also seems to have the login details for her dead fiancé's Instagram account. They've just commented on her most recent post with something that could be interpreted as a threat.'

'Could you be more specific?'

Julia told Sid all about the intruder in her apartment, the burnt dress and the comment from Nicolás's account.

'I'll talk to the victim support unit,' said Sid. 'But I don't think it's enough to qualify for protection, not considering how stretched their resources are right now.'

'Would you like to go to the theatre tonight?'

'To see *The Seagull*? Absolutely.'

'I'll sort the tickets,' she said, trying her best to keep the excitement from her voice.

Twelve

AFTER HER CALL WITH SID, Julia felt strangely restless. She grabbed her cane and walked over to the window, then turned around and headed through to the pantry, turned on the tap and filled a glass before the water had run cold, drinking it so quickly that it spilled down her chin.

Julia returned to her desk, dug Rosmarie Björk's card out of her bag and gave her a call about the latest developments.

The head of security listened carefully as she spoke, and then, as expected, said that while they couldn't cancel the performance, they could beef up security that evening and have a guard keep a close eye on Bianca.

'As I understand it, there's going to be a wrap party afterwards?' said Julia.

'Yes, they usually get together at Frippe's first, then head over to Teatergrillen for a meal. I'll ask the guard to stay with her until she gets home.'

Once they had hung up, Julia called Bianca and asked whether she could get her two tickets for that evening's performance of *The Seagull*.

'No problem. Ooh, how fun! I almost feel nervous now, but I'll sort it.'

'Thanks.'

'They'll be waiting for you at the ticket office. One for you and one for your police contact,' she said in an amused tone of voice.

'Sid.'

'Julia and Sid, Julia and Sid.'

'Bianca, I don't know whether you've seen it already, but one of the comments on your latest Instagram po—'

'Yeah, I saw. It sent a shiver down my spine. Suddenly he's writing messages to me again, as though everything is back to normal? I panicked, deleted it and blocked him.'

'I understand that, but—'

'I took a screenshot.'

'Good, but going forward I'd appreciate it if you would talk to me first.'

'OK, sorry.'

'I spoke to Rosmarie Björk about the threat, in any case, and—'

'What threat?'

'I interpreted his comment as threatening.'

'Did you? Oof ... I mean, I know it was really creepy, but ...'

'Rosmarie is going to ask one of the security guards to stay with you all evening.'

'You've really got me worried now,' said Bianca.

After doing her best to reassure the actress, Julia ended the call and made her way up the stairs to her apartment. She took a shower and then walked naked into her bedroom. She opened the top drawer in her dresser, took out a small tissue-wrapped parcel, tore back the paper and cut the labels from the pretty pale pink underwear.

She had bought them from Fleur du Mal with the intention of wearing them when Sid took her out to dinner, but had changed her mind and decided it would be too humiliating when she inevitably went home alone. But now that she was no longer holding out any hope for him, she reasoned she may as well wear them with the sand-coloured dress that hugged her curves.

Julia headed back through to the bathroom, where she slowly did her makeup. She had been experimenting with a new concealer and foundation lately, to soften the impact of her scars slightly. She added a little blusher, and as she applied her lipstick, it was as though her mother appeared in the mirror.

They really did look alike when she made herself up in this way.

'Hi, Mum . . .'

Julia leaned in and studied her almond-shaped eyes, her deep green irises and the reflection of her face in her dark pupils.

'I know you think I have a foolish heart, and maybe that's true, but I'm not getting carried away. I just want to be close to him for a bit longer, just a little bit . . . before he meets someone he really loves. Someone who puts a stop to it.'

As Julia approached the theatre, she spotted Sid in his creased linen suit among the hundreds of other people waiting on the steps. He looked like he was lost in thought, and she found herself wondering what was on his mind. His face lit up when he saw her, and she felt a jolt of warmth pulse through her heart.

'Did you have your suit on under your uniform all day?' she asked.

'Is it that bad?'

'No,' she replied, trying to hold back a smile.

'Thanks . . . though I can tell that you really mean yes.'

'It's just a bit crumpled, that's all,' she said with a laugh.

They made their way inside, collected the envelope containing their tickets and continued through to the foyer. Sid supported Julia's arm as they climbed the marble steps, but quickly let go of her to check his phone.

The final performance of *The Seagull* was almost sold out, and the only seats Bianca had been able to reserve at such late notice were towards the back of the stalls, at the far right of row seventeen. Julia took the aisle seat to avoid coming into contact with anyone other than Sid.

The murmur from the audience died down a little following the last bell, and Julia gazed out across the heads in front of her, thinking about what Bianca had said about seeing Nicolás in one of the front rows.

If he was still alive, then it was almost certainly him she had seen here, and he who had contacted her via Instagram. But if he was dead, then Bianca had simply been mistaken and the man in the audience likely had nothing to do with her stalker.

Either way, there was a chance that her stalker – whether Nicolás or someone else with a fixation on her – was in the audience tonight. Someone who, using Nicolás's account, had left a threatening comment in order to scare or possibly warn her about what he had planned.

The doors to the foyer closed, and the lighting began to dim. As darkness filled the auditorium, a hush took over.

A violin started playing a melancholy tune, and the lights came up on the stage to reveal the interior of a middle-class home. Through the veranda doors, a cluster of birches was visible in the distance.

Chekhov's infamous gun was mounted on the wall above the dining table.

A naked man wandered across the stage as the screech of a lone gull echoed through the auditorium.

Every fibre of Julia's being was conscious that Sid was sitting beside her in the darkness, and she suddenly found herself thinking back to the time they made love as the clock struck midnight at New Year in Jerusalem.

That's how you do it, she had said afterwards, as they lay side by side, listening to the fireworks slowly petering out.

Neither of them had ever been to Israel before, but they had travelled there with Sid's mother to visit his grandfather and uncle over Hanukkah and Tenth of Tevet.

Following a family dinner on the last day of December, they had gone back to their suite with views out over the Western Wall at the King David Hotel.

They had undressed each other, drunk wine in bed and eaten slices of apple dipped in honey, just like on Rosh Hashana – and the year that followed had been the last sweet one of their lives together.

On a frigid February morning fourteen months later, Julia had made a terrible mistake, one that ruined everything and closed Sid's heart to her.

Back in the theatre, she pressed her thigh against his like some sort of infatuated schoolgirl, just to feel his body heat through her dress.

On the stage, Bianca's performance as the young, bold Nina was utterly heartbreaking.

By the final act, once she had been broken both physically and mentally, people were openly sobbing in the audience.

Konstantin took down the gun from the wall and left the stage.

The show was over, the lights came on, and for a moment or two, there was complete silence, as though all of the air had been sucked out of the theatre. The audience was forced to realise – with a sense of loss and relief – that what they had just experienced was nothing but an act.

And then they burst into rapturous applause.

Bianca's cheeks were streaked with tears as she came back out onto the stage and took a deep bow.

Right then, a man in the third row got to his feet. He was holding a dark green bundle in his arms.

'Sid,' said Julia.

Sid got up, pushed past her and hurried down the aisle.

Julia's heart was racing as the man started making his way out.

Bianca held a hand to her chest and bowed again.

A guard wearing an earpiece was approaching from the left.

The rest of the audience rose in a standing ovation.

The man had now reached the stage.

Sid broke into a run.

Bianca grinned and blew kisses towards the stalls and balcony.

The man pulled back the green tissue paper around a bouquet of red roses right as Sid caught up with him.

Bianca walked over and took the flowers with a huge smile, then returned to the rest of the cast and blew a few more kisses.

Sid led the man off to one side as the applause rose for the director, who had just come out onto the stage.

Thirteen

J ULIA AND SID HUNG BACK in the auditorium, watching
the audience as they filed out towards the cloakrooms.

Sid explained that he had flashed his police badge to
the man with the roses and asked him to show his ID before
he let him go.

'The cast are planning to meet at Frippe's before they go for
dinner at Teatergrillen,' said Julia. 'What do you say, do you
fancy going over there for a glass of wine?'

Sid glanced down at his watch, and because she knew him
better than anyone else on earth, she knew that he needed to
think carefully about how she would interpret his answer.

After she betrayed both him and herself in an unforgivable
way, his passion, love and attraction to her had vanished in an
instant.

All that was now left was pity.

But over the summer, as Julia's birthday approached, she had
come up with a plan to pump some life back into what they
once had.

It was like a narrow chink of light through a tiny window.

Though the prospect terrified her, she had called him and
claimed she needed his professional help with the Mannheim

case. And Sid had proved far more useful than she could ever have expected.

Things had been going pretty well on a personal level, too, though not good enough for her to dare ask if he felt like a change of career.

Julia knew they could make an incredible team.

She was good at reading people, at spotting subtleties beneath the surface, but without Sid by her side she got waylaid much too easily. She had a tendency to get ahead of herself, and her hasty conclusions often ricocheted through the air, hitting innocent bystanders.

'I'm going to head over there, in any case,' Julia said in an attempt to break the silence. 'I want to see how she behaves around the others. I don't know, I often find that sort of thing really helpful, getting a sense of people's interactions before I make my official entrance.'

She wasn't going to nag or start pleading with him. It wasn't true, of course, that he was the only person she was capable of loving, whose touch she could stand – or so she tried to tell herself. There had to be millions of other men she could be happy with, who could take his place.

She had just become fixated on him, it was as simple as that.

Like a stalker, she thought, as she headed for the exit.

'The Mishkan encompasses all creation,' he called after her.

Julia stopped and turned around. Leaning against her cane, she met his amused eye.

'The Mishkan?'

'Yeah,' he replied with a shrug.

'Does that mean you're coming?'

'I have to get up early, but one glass of wine . . .'

Sid and Julia picked a spot by the end of the bar, giving them a good view of the rest of the space. She was sitting on a high stool with her back to the wall, Sid by her side. He was used to acting as a kind of barrier between her and the rest of the world.

They toasted and sipped the Italian wine she had ordered for them.

'Do you really have to get up early, or do you just have other plans this evening?' she asked.

'What am I supposed to say to that?'

'That I should shut up and mind my own bloody business,' she suggested.

'I don't want to do that, but ...'

'Sorry, I'm not sure why I keep saying things I don't mean. I know exactly where we stand, and I genuinely want you to be happy – even if that means cutting me out of your life.'

He looked sad. 'Why do you do this?'

'I'll stop,' she said, taking another sip of wine.

Julia set her glass down on the counter and waited for the wave of anxiety to recede.

She had no idea how long the cast might need to take off their costumes and makeup, shower and get changed, but she planned to use all the time she had to try to undo what she had said and get him to believe that their relationship was strictly professional.

Julia leaned in closer and started telling Sid about her first phone call from Bianca, that it had ended with her getting into a cab and meeting the actress at the 7-Eleven in Nytorget.

When she mentioned that she had searched Bianca's apartment, she saw a flicker of disapproval cross Sid's face.

'There was no one there,' she hurried to add. 'Bianca came in with me, locked the door and immediately tried the handle, which I took as a sign that she's genuinely scared, that the fear has really sunk its teeth into her.'

Julia went on, telling him about the conversation she and Bianca had that night, about the email from Nicolás's mother announcing that he was dead and the fact that his body was immediately flown back to Brazil to be buried, without Biance being given the opportunity to see either him or his death certificate.

'Which could explain why she thinks he's alive,' Sid said with a nod.

Julia agreed, and she continued, talking about the irony of the fact that one of their reasons for getting engaged had been to prevent Bianca from feeling like Nicolás's mistress around his relatives, when ultimately she had been treated like a mistress all the same. Legally, there was nothing tying her to Nicolás, and she had never met his family.

'How much do you know about him?' Sid asked.

'I've only scratched the surface so far,' Julia replied, reaching for her glass again. 'But the Castelo family seem to be pretty influential in Brazil, and they have ties to Sweden going back several generations. Nicolás got his degree from the Stockholm School of Economics, went home to Brazil after he graduated, then came back to Sweden and met Bianca. They lived in some kind of hippy commune with her ex for a year or so before he got a job with the embassy.'

'OK.'

'He was good-looking – though his hair was thinning a bit – always in a dark suit, with cufflinks, a platinum watch and—'

'What kind of watch?' asked Sid.

'A Patek Philippe something-or-other . . .'

'Tourbillon?'

'Exactly.'

'That just means that the watch has a three-dimensional tourbillon,' Sid said.

'OK . . .?' Julia laughed.

'Which is another way of saying that it's got an elaborate mechanical complication inside,' he explained. 'And it counteracts the effects of gravity by having the escapement and balance wheel inside a rotating cage that—'

'OK, thanks.' She cut him off. 'That's enough, Little Robot.'

'It's been a long time since you last called me that,' he said with a smile.

Julia often used to joke that he was her little robot whenever he got too formal or started reeling off unnecessary facts.

'In any case,' she said, trailing a finger around the rim of her glass, 'I talked Bianca into having the locks changed and getting a door guard and peephole fitted, but I think it's probably also time for security cameras and a personal alarm.'

As she spoke, there was a sudden commotion at the other end of the bar.

Julia turned and saw Bianca Salo come in through the doorway with a large group of other people.

The actress looked relaxed, with a light face of makeup and her blonde hair loose. She had pulled on a black leather jacket over her yellow dress, and was deep in animated conversation with a middle-aged man.

Someone took her jacket and hung it up.

The security guard hovering nearby was wearing a tight-fitting navy suit and a pair of black trainers.

Two older women who were drinking white wine at one of the other tables took a couple of snaps of Bianca, only half-heartedly trying to hide what they were doing.

Sid turned so that he could see a little more of the room, following Julia's eye.

Beside Bianca, a man with tattooed arms stood tall and flashed a fake smile at a woman who had gone over to say hello.

'Mikko Järvinen,' Julia mumbled beneath her breath.

'I tried watching his new cop show on TV,' said Sid. 'But I don't know . . .'

'He's basically playing you,' she teased him.

Sid rolled his eyes, and she felt a rush of warmth at having been able to joke with him.

Mikko was a popular actor who did a lot of film and TV work. Julia took in his pale, searching eyes, his alert face and coquettish smile.

'He's got a part in *Macbeth*, too,' she said.

'Two stars on the same stage,' Sid muttered to himself.

Mikko leaned forward and pretended to be interested in Bianca's necklace, but he immediately let go of it and trailed a thumb across her throat. It was clear that Bianca didn't appreciate him touching her, because she shuffled slightly to one side to say something to the older woman who had played Arkadina in *The Seagull*. Mikko's hand moved down to Bianca's bare upper arm, but she almost immediately pulled away to wave to the bartender.

Bianca met Julia's eye, calmly holding her gaze for a moment before moving on to Sid with a flicker of curiosity.

There was a pop, and the actress smiled and turned back to the bartender, who had opened the first bottle of champagne and started filling glasses.

Mikko was drinking a pint of beer, and was now standing much closer to Sid and Julia as he got into conversation with a younger man in a hoodie.

'I was at UFC Fight Night at the weekend,' they heard him say. 'Sitting right by the cage ... Alexander Weston's a buddy of mine. I swear, the guy's lethal. Won on submission, the other bloke was just screaming.'

Julia noticed that Sid had a gleam in his eye, that one corner of his mouth had started to twitch. She put a reassuring hand on his forearm, and he nodded to her.

He had always found the kind of cocksure men who talked up their own manliness so ridiculous that he sometimes broke down in an uncontrollable fit of laughter. It bubbled up like a volcanic eruption and typically ended with him laughing so hard that he couldn't breathe and having to lie down on the floor.

Mikko rolled his shoulders like a boxer and held up his fist for the other man to see, pointing at his knuckles.

'Don't look at him,' Julia warned Sid.

'No,' he replied, fanning himself with one hand.

'Shall we go?' Julia asked, getting down from her stool.

'I can do this.'

She saw that his mouth had started twitching again and realised he would probably start laughing at any moment.

'Don't listen to him, listen to me,' she said.

Small beads of sweat were now glistening on Sid's forehead, soft whimpering sounds escaping from his mouth.

'I actually trained with Alexander Weston for a while,' Mikko continued. 'He says I've got it. Y'know, it's all in the eyes ... He says I could go far.'

Julia gripped Sid's face with both hands, stood on her tiptoes and kissed him square on the lips.

Fourteen

THE NEXT MORNING, JULIA STARK made her way back to the Royal Dramatic Theatre. She was wearing an ochre blazer and skirt, and the warm colour brought out the reddish hue in her hair and eyebrows.

It was forecast to be another warm day. People would no doubt flock to the coast, and the parks would be full of picnic blankets and baskets, playing children and sunbathing teenagers.

Julia stuck to the shady side of Riddargatan. She could smell freshly baked sourdough and coffee from the cafés, and when she glanced down towards Nybroviken as she passed the side streets, she saw the water glittering and gulls circling over the white boats.

That morning, when she woke, she saw that she had a brief text message from Bianca, sent in the middle of the night:

Saw you and Sid at the bar. The two of you look good together, super hot;)

Julia had slumped back against the pillow, closed her eyes and tried to compose herself. Her kiss had saved Sid from a fit of laughter, but it had also unsettled him, and he had mumbled that he had to get up early, paid for their drinks and left.

Julia paused, rummaged through her bag and took out her phone.

He still hadn't called or texted.

She would have liked to talk to him about the list of people who were at the theatre when Bianca's dress caught fire. The incident had taken place fairly late in the day, so it was a relatively small group of just ninety-eight people.

According to the security system, only seventeen actors, dressers and directors had accessed her corridor. None of them had a key to the dressing room, but as Bianca herself had admitted, that door was almost always left unlocked.

Other than Ramon, the whole cast of *Macbeth* had been present for a workshop.

Five performers from *The Seagull* had also been on the corridor, along with two dressers and three actors from a production on one of the smaller stages.

As Julia walked beneath the glass skyway that connected the two buildings housing the various auditoriums, she reminded herself that Bianca's stalker wasn't necessarily one of the names on the list. But if that was the case, whoever it was had managed to completely bypass the theatre's security systems.

She made her way inside and over to the artfully lit reception area. Behind the gently curved marble-topped desk, there was a panel of walnut wood. Julia showed the receptionist her ID, signed for her electronic key pass, and asked the way to rehearsal room two.

She listened to the directions, thanked the woman for her help and headed through a set of polished brass and glass doors to the left of reception.

The stone floor in the backstage area was well-worn, as though she was in some sort of industrial building, and the walls, doors and metal trims were all scuffed and dented.

Julia stepped into the right-hand lift, scanned her security pass and pressed the button for the fifth floor.

As it carried her upwards, she thought about how calmly Bianca had dealt with Mikko's unwanted advances, without causing a scene.

Julia herself had something bordering on a phobia of unexpected physical contact. A hand on her bare shoulder could send a wave of post-traumatic shock through her, a panicked reminder of wet body parts against her skin, of trying to hold together the edges of a wound that was slick with blood.

She had no idea what to expect from a theatre rehearsal, and suddenly started worrying that the cast might try to involve her in some sort of physical game or teambuilding exercise.

The lift doors opened with a screech, and Julia stepped out into a corridor. She paused and leaned against her cane for a moment, wondering whether she was on the right floor.

The space in front of her looked like a deserted office, with a grey carpet, aluminium air vents on the ceiling and various cables coated with decades' worth of paint.

She started walking, passing a small seating area in an alcove. It was full of mismatched furniture, with a bobbled rainbow cushion on one of the chairs, a coffee machine on top of a small fridge and rings left by cups and glasses on the simple wooden tables.

Julia thought back to her conversation with Tommy Roos in the staff canteen. He had mentioned that Nicolás punched Mikko just a few days before he died.

But the subtext to what he had said was that nothing ever changes.

It was as though Tommy's lived experience had cost him more than it had given back, Julia thought as she walked down a corridor of closed doors, stacked chairs and moving boxes.

On a half-open door flecked with white paint, someone had taped a laminated sheet of paper marked 'Rehearsal Room 2'.

Being able to pinpoint a time and place was one of the key steps in identifying who might have had the opportunity to commit the crime in question.

Someone had set fire to Bianca's dress between 9 and 10 p.m. on Thursday night.

The person responsible had been in her dressing room at that particular point in time.

Even if there were no witnesses to the incident itself, someone might have seen something of note either before or after.

So although the actual timeframe was fairly narrow, Julia would need to widen it if she wanted to try to find some trace of the perpetrator's entry or exit.

It could be the case that some of the artistic staff had arrived early or stayed later than usual, that a journalist or private guest had been present, a transport company or florist, cleaning staff or a handyman changing a filter in the ventilation system.

Both Regina and Tommy had said that they hadn't seen anything out of the ordinary last week, but neither had really taken the time to consider the question.

Julia would have to speak to them again.

A person's memory often needed a helping hand to click into gear. Someone to take the controls for a moment, giving them time to process everything anew.

Julia used her cane to push the door open and walked through into a large room with a long table in the middle of the black floor. Daylight flooded into the space through three windows in the sloping ceiling, which was fitted with acoustic panels and black light fittings.

Of the six people inside, she had already met three.

Bianca's pale skin and bright red lips made her look like a silent film star. She had her blonde hair tied up in a high ponytail, and she was wearing a black polo neck and a pair of black trousers, clutching the script to her chest as she talked to Regina Muhammed.

As before, the director's grey hair was gathered in a loose plait. She had on a pair of oversized glasses, a knitted dress and cardigan, black tights and low shoes.

She seemed to be treating Bianca with some sort of anxious attentiveness, straightening her collar, pushing back a lock of hair from her forehead and gripping her slim shoulders.

The young actor Ramon Breiner was in front of the mirror, performing a series of pirouettes like a trained ballet dancer, his eyes fixed on the same spot for turn after turn.

Tommy Roos was chatting to two women over by the piano.

Bianca noticed Julia and waved, and Julia walked over and paused around two metres away.

'Hey, good-looking,' Bianca said with a bright smile.

'How did it feel to sleep at home last night?' Julia asked.

'Good,' she replied, though she immediately blushed.

Julia turned to the director.

'Regina, I really appreciate you letting me be here today.'

'Of course.'

'You're going to love it,' said Bianca. 'This bunch ... We're like a big family – with everything that entails.'

'Mikko's the only one not here yet,' said Regina. 'Plus a minor triple role who can't make it today.'

'OK,' said Julia, turning to the women who were chatting to Tommy Roos.

'That's our prompter, Ursula Andersson, and our stage manager, Anna Dagerman,' Regina explained. 'Costume and set design will be stopping by later, too.'

A loud, high note rang out as Tommy pressed the top key on the piano and turned away from the two women. He came over to join Julia, Bianca and Regina. He had dark circles beneath his eyes, and his greying hair was messy.

'Strange to see Ursula again,' he said quietly.

'Tommy's like an encyclopaedia of the Swedish theatre world. Our most experienced actor, no doubt about it,' said Bianca, patting him on the back.

'Which is her way of saying that I'm ancient,' he shot back with a smile.

Bianca laughed. 'He's done everything, worked with everyone ...'

'He was even Ingmar Bergman's private punching bag,' said Regina.

'Ingmar was an extreme power-seeker ... He wanted to be a cult leader, not a minister like his daddy,' Tommy attempted to explain to Julia. 'He could be a real bastard, but I took it because I knew he needed me.'

'Yeah, and you ended up on the psych ward, but sure ...' Regina muttered.

'I was just burnt out,' he said with a broken smile before making his way over to the table.

Fifteen

IANCA TORE HER EYES AWAY from Tommy, but she didn't manage to banish the troubled look from her face until Regina apologised and took out her phone. 'Hey, have you seen Mikko?' the director asked the person on the other end. 'He isn't picking up, and we've technically already started the first read-through in room two ... Right, OK, I'll talk to Göran.'

Regina walked away with her phone to her ear.

'I feel like I should apologise,' said Bianca. 'Everyone always gets a bit stressed out when Mikko is involved. He forgets about rehearsals, walks out in the middle of them ...'

Ramon drew the black curtain across the large mirror.

Julia moved a step closer to Bianca. 'I had a quick chat with Tommy yesterday,' she said, keeping her voice low. 'He mentioned that Nicolás and Mikko got into a fight at a bar.'

Bianca chewed on her lower lip and nodded. 'I'm not sure I'd call it a fight, but yeah. It was pretty bad. Nicolás marched right up to him and smacked him in the face.'

'Why?'

'It's complicated,' she replied wearily.

'Jealousy?'

'Nicolás was a Catholic, and he struggled with the idea of me running about half-naked on stage every day. He dealt with it, for the most part, but with Mikko it was—'

'OK, everyone, shall we get started?' Regina shouted.

'What were you going to say?' asked Julia.

'Just that things were a bit tense,' Bianca replied.

'Why?'

'I don't have time to get into it now.'

'What do you keep in your safe?' Julia pressed her.

The actress seemed taken aback by the sudden change of subject. 'At home? A few bits of jewellery, my passport, the deeds for the apartment.'

'To do with Nicolás, I mean.'

'Oof,' said Bianca, her cheeks flushing. 'OK, look ... A few days after he died, I got a letter from Helsinki.'

'From Nicolás?'

'Yeah.'

'What did it say?'

'I don't know, I never opened it. On the contrary ... I panicked, didn't want to know, so I locked it away.'

'Come and sit down, please,' Regina shouted, clapping her hands.

'Can I read it?' asked Julia.

'I can't do this, not now.'

Everyone took their seats around the table, with the prompter and the stage manager at the opposite end to the actors. Julia moved a little closer, then paused and leaned against her cane. She studied Ramon Breiner in profile. He was wearing dark blue sports trousers and a grey hoodie, and the expression on his face reminded her of a purring cat. Bianca switched her phone to silent, put an arm around his shoulders and whispered something in his ear.

Regina had just taken a deep breath to start talking when Mikko Järvinen strode into the room.

'Is it me you've been waiting for?' he asked, pausing in front of the table with a grin. 'Shit, it's great to see you all again!'

He started making his way around the others, greeting each of them in turn. He hugged Regina, ruffled Tommy's hair and patted Ramon on the shoulder.

'Darling!'

Mikko leaned in and kissed Bianca on the neck, then wrapped his arms around her, his right hand cupping her left breast. Ramon lowered his eyes and stared down at the table with gritted teeth.

'Sit down, please, Mikko,' Regina said flatly.

He straightened up, walked over to Julia and studied her scar. 'That real?'

'Yes,' she replied, gripping her cane in both hands.

'Sorry, that was insensitive of me,' he said with a smile.

'No harm done,' she said, conscious that her heart was racing out of fear that he might touch her.

'Sit down, Mikko,' Regina repeated. 'Now.'

Mikko turned away from Julia and sat down at the table, leaning back in his chair with a satisfied look on his face.

'Feel free to sit wherever you like, Julia,' said the director.

'Thank you,' she said, taking a seat as far away from the others as she could.

'OK, everyone, welcome. This is going to be really bloody fun,' Regina began. 'As you might have noticed, Bianca has a guest today . . . Shall I explain, or do you want to do it yourself?'

'No, I can do it,' said Bianca, raising a hand. 'I've hired a private detective who—'

Mikko laughed.

'Whose name is Julia Stark.'

'Seriously?' he said with a forced smile.

'Julia was the one who solved the china dolls case.'

'Respect.'

'She's going to be joining us today, and possibly at a few more rehearsals going forward, if that's OK.'

'Depends what she's investigating,' Mikko said hesitantly.

Regina waved her hand to give Julia the floor.

'It seems as though Bianca has a stalker,' Julia began. 'Which isn't especially uncommon, particularly not for people as well-known as all of you . . . But the real issue is that Bianca's stalker also seems to be in an escalatory spiral at the moment, and has broken into both her home and her dressing room.'

'Here?'

'Yes.'

'Is he dangerous?' asked Mikko.

'I don't want to make any assumptions to the contrary,' she replied. 'Which is why I'm trying to stick as close to Bianca as I can, and I'd—'

'Sorry, but you don't exactly look like a bodyguard,' Ramon spoke up.

'No. I'm the one who gets to the bottom of whatever is going on,' she said. 'I'm the one who will find the stalker and make sure he or she is brought to justice.'

'Right.'

'And that's why I'd like to talk to each of you individually,' she continued. 'As you all know, memory is an incredibly complex thing. In response to a direct question, most people will reply that they didn't see anything out of the ordinary on Thursday evening, but I'd still like to start by asking you just that.'

Time seemed to slow right down, the ticking of her father's old watch becoming increasingly sluggish. Julia lost contact with the seat beneath her, her eardrums curved inwards, and the familiar feeling of weightlessness and crystalline focus took hold.

'Anyone see anything?' Mikko asked the rest of the room.

'Nope,' said Ramon.

'It's 9 p.m.,' said Julia, licking her lips. 'A performance of *The Seagull* is currently underway on the main stage. It's the interval, which means the foyers are all full of people. Where were each of you?'

'Anyone who wasn't on stage was taking part in a workshop on the sixteenth century,' said Regina.

Julia felt as though she had stepped outside of herself, as though there was some sort of rag doll in her seat, a recording of her voice playing through its fabric chest.

'Take yourselves back to that evening, really think,' the doll said without moving its lips. 'Mikko, did you see anything? Tommy?'

As she continued to talk, she gazed at the people around the table.

Ramon's eyes had narrowed, and he kept sniffing to stop his nose from running. He looked as though he couldn't quite decide what to make of the private detective and her questions.

The tip of Bianca's tongue was poking out between her lips.

Mikko looked more amused than anything, his reaction hovering somewhere between over-confidence and arrogance.

Tommy didn't seem to have been listening at all, nodding to himself and staring at nothing in particular with a blank look on his face.

'You might have seen something important.'

Bianca looked both pleased and deliberately anxious.

'Possibly without even realising it,' the doll continued.

A flicker of impatience had appeared on Regina's face, but she regained her usual warmth the minute she realised that Julia had no intention of taking up any more time.

Julia felt a slight tingle between her legs as she came back down to earth, and she rubbed her lips with a trembling hand.

'Before we really get stuck into rehearsals, I'd like to leave you all with one little bit of fluff,' Regina said with a smile. 'You're not a drop in the ocean. You're the entire ocean ... in a single drop.'

Sixteen

A S REGINA BRIEFED THE CAST on a few important changes to the rehearsal schedule, Bianca got up, walked over to the water cooler and started filling glasses at the little tap.

'We've got Jocke working on the set this time, which is cool. He said he'd try to swing by after lunch.'

Bianca flitted back and forth between the cooler and the table, setting the glasses of water down in front of her colleagues. Julia was the only one who seemed to be paying any attention to what she was doing. After filling the last glass, Bianca turned around and spat into it before handing it to Mikko and taking her seat again.

Mikko's face was aged and weary, but in a handsome, melancholic way. His pale eyes were slightly glassy, like those of someone who had drunk a serious amount of alcohol over a long period of time, and he had a large plaster around his wrist and deep white scars on the knuckles of his right hand.

Tommy Roos kept smiling, as though he was posing for a photo shoot he didn't quite have the energy for.

'As ever, let's avoid using the name of the tragedy other than in direct address,' said Regina, holding up a stack of scripts.

'Great,' said Tommy.

Bianca exchanged an amused look with Julia.

'I've never really understood that superstitious stuff,' said Mikko. 'Saying Hamlet, Othello or King Lear is fine, but one mention of the M-word and everyone shits themselves.'

'Legend has it that, despite warnings, Shakespeare used spells belonging to three real-life witches,' Regina explained. 'And they responded by putting a curse on the play, one that means any theatre where the name is uttered will be struck by tragedy.'

'What name?' Bianca asked with a grin.

'Of the tragedy.'

'I can't remember it. Can someone remind me?'

'Just like last time, we've got a few double and triple roles,' Regina continued unperturbed. 'Kerstin couldn't make it today, so I'll be reading her lines. Ignore the stage directions and all that jazz – you know the play and your parts from last time. I just want us all to get a feel for the text again. It's been a few years, which means we'll be stepping into the roles as new people. Calmly, without any rush.'

'I love this,' Bianca said with a smile.

Julia noticed that the actors all seemed to be handling their scripts with real affection, stroking the reams of paper, fingers lingering on the pages.

Regina flicked forward to the first act, cleared her throat and started reading the witches' dialogue:

"*When shall we three meet again? In thunder, lightning, or in rain?*'
'*When the hurly-burly's done, when the battle's lost and won.*'"

Once the witches had exited the stage, it was Tommy Roos's turn. He was playing Duncan, King of Scotland, who had just come face-to-face with a wounded soldier.

"'What bloody man is that?'" Tommy read. *"'He can report, as seemeth by his plight, of the revolt the newest state.'"*

"'This is the sergeant who, like a good and hardy soldier, fought 'gainst my captivity,'" Ramon replied in a soft voice.

As they continued, a heavy silence settled around them, as though the room itself was holding its breath. The artless way they were performing the play gave it a certain austerity, a pared-back sense of heading for the abyss. Julia's senses were heightened, and she felt a vague sense of dread fill the rehearsal space. With that, she realised she had caught a glimpse of the essence of the drama: the birth of a killer.

Bianca knew her lines so well that she stopped turning the page in her script, though she still made sure to deliver them without emotion, as though she was reading them for the very first time.

"'How tender 'tis to love the babe that milks me. I would, while it was smiling in my face, have plucked my nipple from his boneless gums and dashed the brains out, had I so sworn as you have done to this.'"

Mikko took a deep breath and glanced at her.

"'If we should fail—'" he began.

"'We fail?'" Bianca replied. *"'But screw your courage to the sticking place and we'll not fail.'"*

The sunlight flooding in through the skylights slowly drifted across the floor, and as they approached the climax of the tragedy it reached the mixing console, illuminating the faders and dials, the cables and computer.

Julia saw the hair on Bianca's arms stand on end as the doctor and the gentlewoman started talking over her Lady Macbeth.

"Infected minds to their deaf pillows will discharge their secrets," said Ramon. *"More needs she the divine than the physician. God, God forgive us all."*

The prompter, who had been following every line with the tip of her pen, smiled for the first time.

One actor's voice gave way to another, and the meter and rhyme became almost hypnotic as they reached the closing scene, where Macbeth lay dead and Scotland had a new king.

After the read-through was over, they all sat in silence for a moment or two. Regina slowly closed her script and looked up.

'Thank you,' she said quietly. 'You're ... you're all wonderful. This is going to be magical. Magnificent.'

Seventeen

THE CAST GOT UP FROM the table and scattered around the room. Julia watched Regina and Mikko disappear through the doorway, and the prompter went and sat down at the production desk with her folder. Bianca gave Ramon's hand a squeeze before hurrying away, and Tommy followed the technician over to the mixing console, let out a flattered laugh and opened his little tub of snus.

'It's like stage fright,' Julia heard him say. 'Some people draw strength from it, but others suffer like crazy – just take Greta Garbo or Per Oscarsson, who refused to accept that his entrance was coming up. He started talking about going out to get a hot dog, and the stage manager had to physically push him out onto the stage at the exact right moment. Once he was out there, of course, he was always incredible, but still.'

The lighting tech laughed and moved off to one side to take a phone call, pausing by the spiral staircase.

'Tommy, could I have a quick word?' asked Julia, getting up and moving over to him. 'I noticed that you nodded when I mentioned that someone might have seen something on Thursday evening.'

'Did I?' he asked.

'Yes.'

'I didn't realise.'

'Were you at the workshop?'

'No, I had a small part in *The Seagull*. Yakov, a workman. Look, I don't want to get mixed up in whatever this is, but during the interval I did see a bag on the floor in our corridor.'

'Where?'

'By the wall near the loo.'

'Did you look inside?'

'Yeah, it was a bottle of Absolut Vodka.'

'Whose?'

'No idea,' he said, turning and leaving the room.

Julia steadied herself with her cane and looked up at the blue sky through one of the skylights.

Ramon sat down at the piano, placed some music in front of him and started playing a piece from Verdi's *Macbeth*.

Julia moved closer to listen.

On top of the piano, there was a yellow warning sticker. There should be a piano available in every rehearsal room, it said. Anyone found in violation of that rule would be punished by being given a one-year membership to Stockholm City Theatre.

'You're a man of many talents,' she said once the last note had faded.

'For someone from the hood, you mean?'

'Are you?'

Ramon flashed her a cute smile and then gave a head wobble in reply.

'You and Bianca seem to have a close relationship ... New, but close,' she continued.

He raised an eyebrow. 'Very observant.'

'You have no idea.'

'OK.'

'That wasn't a threat,' she said with a smile. 'Just an observation.' He nodded.

'In all honesty, I'm feeling the pressure a bit. We need to find Bianca's stalker, and fast,' said Julia, studying him closely.

'You don't *seem* like you're under pressure.'

'Have you seen anything you think I should know about?'

Ramon shrugged and played a few high notes from *Romeo and Juliet* with his left hand.

'People stare at her wherever she goes,' he said. 'They whisper, take photos, pretend they don't recognise her and strike up conversations. They send letters, flowers, gifts.'

'Anything that sticks out?'

'A woman with a cane who can't tear her eyes away from her.'

'Did you know her fiancé?' asked Julia.

'Not really, but I did meet him a couple of times.'

'I heard about the fight just before he died ...'

'From Bianca?'

'Were you there?'

'Yeah.'

'Was Nicolás jealous?'

'Why would he be?' Ramon smirked. 'Mikko was at the top of his game. A famous actor, a sex symbol. The guy got every part he wanted, and Bianca had sex with him in a bathroom just to get her foot in the door here.'

'How do you know that?'

'Everyone knows. Even Nicolás knew, apparently ... Scratch the surface a little. It's really not a big deal here that some people—'

He stopped himself.

'What were you going to say?' asked Julia.

Ramon sighed. 'Look, I know how it sounds, like Bianca slept her way to where she is now, but I swear, she didn't. She's worked harder than most. It's just that sometimes sex is literally the only way in – for women, I mean. Which is obviously terrible.'

'And for men?'

'Ha,' he said. 'Unless we're worshipped as young gods, we've got to be best pals with the directors and producers. We've got to drink beer and hit the gym.'

'Hard lines,' Julia mumbled.

'Yup.'

He lowered his eyes to the keys.

'So what happened during the fight at the bar?'

'We'd been rehearsing on the main stage, going commando. It was late, and we all ended up at Riche and—'

Ramon paused when Regina came back into the room carrying a cup of coffee and a vegan lunch from the vending machine in the basement.

'We'll start again in fifteen,' she said as she sat down at the table.

'I need to try to get hold of my yoga teacher,' Ramon told Julia.

With that, he got up from the piano and hurried towards the door.

The young man seemed to have some sort of dangerous hunger that was focused on Bianca. Something unrequited, insatiable. The next time they spoke, Julia thought as she walked over to the prompter, she would have to try to find out what was going on beneath the seemingly calm surface.

Ursula Andersson was still sitting at the production desk with the prompt book and a pencil case in front of her. Seeing her up close, Julia realised she was actually very pretty, with sleek brown hair, amber eyes and full lips. But her face was also etched with fine lines, as though she had spent too much of her life crying. She was wearing a long skirt and a grey cardigan with thinning elbows, plus a necklace of two interlinked Venus symbols.

'Hi,' Julia said as she pulled out a chair. 'I've been going around, speaking to everyone, and I was wondering if you saw anything that might be connected to Bianca's stalker last week.'

'Like what?' Ursula asked, in a strangely quiet voice.

'It could have been someone in the corridor who shouldn't have been there, an open door, a strange smell, odd behaviour. Anything, really.'

'I don't know . . .'

'Let's start with the general mood. Has everyone been their usual selves these past few weeks?' Julia asked as she sat down.

'It's been a long time since I last worked here, but the cast does feel a bit nervous,' said Ursula, popping a throat sweet into her mouth.

'More than usual?'

'I'd say so,' she said, clearing her throat.

'Anything else?'

'I saw Mikko coming out of Bianca's dressing room last week,' she said, in a voice that had turned raspy.

'Which day was this?'

'Thursday, I think.'

'Try to remember – was it definitely Thursday?'

'Yes,' Ursula replied after a few seconds.

'What was he doing?'

The prompter took a deep breath and looked around.

'What they get up to is their business, but I saw him shoving a pair of knickers into his pocket . . . He looked like one of those men sneaking out of a porno cinema, if you know what I mean.'

'I think so,' said Julia. 'What did you make of that?'

'No, nothing. Forget I said anything.'

'Do you remember the time?'

'It was evening, but I'm not sure. Sorry, I really need to get back to work,' she said, turning to her script.

'Have you seen anything else that—'

'No.' Ursula cut her off, looking deep into Julia's eyes.

'Well, keep it in mind, for Bianca's sake. Just let me know if you think of anything – anything at all,' Julia said as she got up.

Regina had stopped eating, and was looking down at her phone with a frown. Julia walked over to her and took her seat again.

'I was talking to Tommy about the last time you rehearsed this play,' she said.

'Mmm,' Regina replied, licking her teeth.

'He mentioned a fight between Mikko and Bianca's fiancé.'

'Right, I'd almost forgotten, everything was so chaotic then. Pre-show nerves, you know? Everyone does things they wouldn't otherwise. I spat in Tommy's face, Ramon flipped out and smashed a table with a fire extinguisher, Mikko turned up drunk to the dress rehearsal, and Ursula had some sort of weird auto-immune reaction and ended up in A&E. Then Nicolás died in Helsinki, we got absolutely panned in every review, Bianca had a breakdown and the run was cancelled . . . Maybe you can see why I love the theatre?'

Eighteen

THE HUGE BUILDING COMPLEX THAT housed both the Police Authority and Stockholm Police also contained a swimming pool. It was primarily intended for the officers' life-saving training sessions, but was also open to the general public. In the evenings, members of the police force could book it for private use.

At one point in time, Julia and Sidney used to have the pool to themselves two nights a week, then go out for a late dinner at one of the restaurants nearby.

Julia's body was covered in pale scars, her skin like some sort of badly wiped chalkboard, but Sid had never been embarrassed by the way she looked.

Swimming was the only form of exercise that enabled her to move naturally, but because she couldn't stand the whispering or the stolen glances at regular public baths, she had made do with walking and physiotherapy during the years she couldn't ask Sid for any favours.

Three hours ago, out of the blue, he had sent her a text message asking if she wanted him to book the pool that evening.

Julia knew he wouldn't be swimming himself, that they wouldn't use the sauna together or go out to eat afterwards, but his unexpected message made her so happy that she felt butterflies in her stomach.

Sid met her by the entrance, and they walked through to the women's changing room together. He stood with his back to her as she got changed, but their conversation still felt a little stilted until she had pulled on her pale yellow swimsuit – one he had given her – and wrapped a towel around her hips.

She left her cane in the changing room and held Sid's arm as they came out into the damp, chlorine-scented pool hall. There was no one else around, and all she could hear was the water lapping softly against the overflow drains. The surface of the pool was calm, disturbed only by the barely visible currents from the circulation system.

Julia draped her towel over the back of a bench and started telling Sid about Bianca's case. She said that she didn't like letting the actress out of her sight, but that Bianca was going out for dinner with Regina that evening, then staying over at her place.

'It's actually kind of hard to keep up,' Julia continued, walking over to the edge of the pool. 'I need to get security cameras installed at Bianca's place, and to find out what happened to her fiancé in Helsinki – ideally by getting hold of a death certificate and coroner's report.'

'You should hire someone,' said Sid.

'I know. I was actually planning to ask if—'

'Hold on,' he said when his work phone started ringing.

Sid answered the call, listened for a moment, gave a brief response, listened again and then said he would come right away.

'Sorry,' he told Julia. 'I've got to go.'

'Of course.'

'I'll come back and put the alarm on later, just make sure the door locks behind you when you leave,' he said as he hurried off towards the changing rooms.

'Be careful!' she called after him, though she knew he was already out of earshot.

Julia stood still for a moment, gazing down at the blue tiles and the slowly wavering line markings, then she pulled on her black swim cap and pushed a few stray locks of hair beneath the silicone.

She walked over to the ladder, adjusted her goggles, got into the pool and pushed away from the edge.

Julia glided through the water, just beneath the surface. She kicked twice at double speed, before settling into a crawl at a slower, more efficient rhythm, perfect for long distances. Her elbow rose up out of the water, followed by her forearm, stretching out and breaking the surface ahead of her without a splash, pulling herself forward as the other arm repeated the same movement.

Julia kept an eye on the tiles on the bottom of the pool as she swam, registering the dark blue lane markers and the line letting her know it was almost time to turn, two more strokes before she tumbled round and kicked off.

Her forehead cut through the water, and she heard a roar in her ears. It was as though she became weightless and time disappeared, and she started thinking about Ursula's croaky voice, about how painful it sounded for her to speak. Julia had noticed that the prompter had tears in her eyes as she raised her voice to make herself heard.

Ursula had also started breathing more heavily as she spoke about seeing Mikko come out of Bianca's dressing room.

He had been holding a pair of knickers, she said.

Did he take them as a kind of trophy, or just to be cruel?

It was hard to believe that he and Bianca were in any kind of sexual relationship, after all.

Julia sped through the water, body twisting from side to side. She took a breath every four strokes, thinking about how Ursula had likened Mikko to a man sneaking out of a porno movie, in the moment of transition between the private and public realm.

Her heart had reached a fast, steady rate.

Oxygen flooded to her muscles.

Julia felt strong, like she could keep going forever, and she turned and pushed away from the wall, shooting through the water like a projectile and breaking the surface without losing her rhythm.

She had only swum around eight hundred metres when she heard a muffled voice. It was nothing but a vague, dream-like rumble at first, but then it cut through to her like a howling dog, paws thudding against a closed door.

She felt a jolt of anxiety and stopped swimming, treading water as her heart pounded and her eyes scanned the room. A man in white clothing was standing at the end of the pool.

'Hello!' he shouted.

Julia pulled off her goggles and felt the weight of her blood-filled muscles.

'What the hell d'you think you're playing at? The pool's closed!'

'But I booked—'

'No one's booked anything, what're you on about? I'm here to change the filter and do the backwash.'

She swam over to the edge.

The man was in his fifties, with a sparse beard and a pot belly. He walked around to her, wiping his hands on his white T-shirt, which had the words 'Pool Guys' printed in blue across the chest.

'There must have been some sort of mix-up, because I—'

'Out, right now,' he snapped.

Julia climbed the ladder, water pouring off her body. She was well aware that her swimsuit became slightly see-through when it was wet, that her nipples were visible through the yellow fabric.

'What the hell . . .?' he muttered, stopping dead when he saw her scars.

Julia limped over to the bench, grabbed her towel and hurried through to the changing room without looking back.

She felt so uneasy that she didn't bother to shower, just dried herself off, got dressed and grabbed her cane.

As she came out into the lobby and was making her way over to the door, she heard footsteps behind her.

'Wait, please . . .'

She turned around and saw the man.

'Sorry, you were right. I'd missed the booking,' he said with an apologetic smile. 'Just trying to do my job, y'know? You can keep swimming if you—'

But Julia didn't reply, she just hurried over to the door and left the building.

Once she got home, Julia took a shower, put on a pair of silk pyjamas and made herself a late dinner. She had bought six hundred grams of wagyu beef, enough for two people, and had left the meat to marinate for five hours. She froze half and used the remainder to make yakiniku, with kimchi and jasmine rice. Julia took her time, setting the table with a pale grey plate, chopsticks and a grey linen napkin. She then lit a candle, poured herself a glass of wine, switched her phone to silent and sat down. As she ate, she watched the young couple with a baby that never seemed to sleep in the apartment on the other side of the street.

'All the things that never happen,' she mumbled to her reflection in the window.

Following a long hospital stay involving multiple operations, reconstructions and physiotherapy sessions, Julia had lived on her parents' savings and the compensation paid out by the airline. She took medication and received psychiatric help, but also found herself gripped by nightmares, panic attacks and feelings of guilt.

Little by little, she had frittered the money away, buying things she didn't need and drinking expensive wines. She forgot to pay the bills, gave to charity and was tricked out of a large sum by a man she was involved with.

Romantic relationships had always been incredibly difficult for her, largely because physical touch provoked feelings of deep anxiety, and the unexpected sensation of someone else's skin against hers was a powerful trigger for her PTSD.

Julia had been with a total of nine men and two women over the years, but prior to meeting Sid she had only enjoyed the experience a handful of times. For the most part, sex felt more like an assault than anything, leading to panic attacks if she didn't drink to the point of unconsciousness first.

Despite that, she knew it wasn't impossible for her to enjoy being intimate with someone; there had been one occasion where she was completely present during sex, and had felt both aroused and euphoric. It happened the summer she turned twenty, at a forest rave with her friends. As a light dawn rain fell, she had dragged a man away from the music and the lights, to a quiet glade.

By the time Julia was twenty-two, all the money was gone and she was forced to give up the heavily mortgaged family home. She put everything she had left into storage and started from scratch in a small apartment in Södertälje.

With time, Julia had come to see that moment as a key part of her grieving process. She had needed to lose everything in order to rebuild herself.

She had originally wanted to follow in her mother's footsteps to become a judge, but found she couldn't focus on her studies and had to take several leaves of absence. In the end, she accepted that she would likely have to temper her ambitions. She was no longer a model student, and would probably never outshine her parents.

Julia was working as a secretary at Stockholm District Court when, during a hearing, she saw a police officer called Sidney Mendelson to stand. He looked tired, had come straight from a shift, and was wearing muddy shoes.

He was in court because two of his colleagues had attempted to talk to a young Moroccan man following a fight outside a bar. According to their version of events, the man had become violent and attacked them, and he was then arrested and taken into custody.

The Moroccan man had filed a complaint, and the two officers had filed a counter-complaint in return, claiming that one of them had been so badly injured that she was forced to take time off work.

It was clear what was expected of Sidney, but he had seen some of the incident from a surveillance car and testified in support of the Moroccan. The young man claimed he had nothing to do with the fight, and that he was simply queueing up to get inside and see his girlfriend when the two officers tackled him to the ground, frisked him and assaulted him – purely for asking why.

As he was wrapping up, Sidney had said that while everyone makes mistakes – that doing so was human – he had always had an issue with so many members of the police force filing counter complaints as a matter of course, purely to avoid the repercussions of having used excessive force.

Nineteen

JULIA STARK STEPPED OUT OF the lift on the fifth floor of the theatre building and made her way down the corridor. Her cane thudded softly against the grey wall-to-wall carpet. Someone had left a white extension lead on the sofa, and there was a hole punch and two coffee cups on the low table.

She passed the closed door to rehearsal room two and saw a pair of trainers that had been dumped in a rubbish bin.

At the end of the corridor, a sheet of paper reading 'Rehearsal Room 1' had been taped up beside the green emergency exit sign above the doorway.

The red bulb that could be turned on to indicate that a rehearsal was underway was currently switched off.

Julia walked up the creaky ramp, down a crooked passageway and into the room.

She found everyone but Mikko standing on the worn black stage, deep in conversation about the text and the Swedish translation.

Today Bianca was wearing black tracksuit bottoms and a sweatshirt a pair of white dance shoes on her feet, and a pink scarf tied around her neck.

A tall woman in jeans and a denim jacket was eating an apple with her back to the others.

Julia made her way around the edge of the stage to a small set of stairs that led down to floor level. Regina was sitting behind the production desk over by the row of small windows.

The prompter and stage manager were by the mixing console, talking to a man with blue hair who was busy adjusting the lights on the stage.

Regina's bracelets clinked as she waved for Julia to come over.

'You can sit here, if you like,' she said.

'Thank you,' Julia replied, taking a seat beside her.

Regina had just started to explain that the rehearsal room was the exact same size as the main stage when she was suddenly interrupted by a loud scraping sound.

Mikko came into the room pulling a black chair behind him. He paused in the middle of the stage, sat down and grinned at the other actors.

Like a king on his throne, Julia thought.

Regina got to her feet and went up onto the stage. 'As I see it – if you'll allow me to be pompous for a moment – our greatest asset is also our greatest vulnerability . . .' she said, eyes lingering on her cast. 'Everyone here already knows their part inside out, and it's that impression that we need to pare back. We need to pare back everything but the words if we're going to find a new route into the tragedy . . . otherwise we don't deserve a second chance.'

'Is that even possible?' Bianca asked with a smile.

'Yes,' said Regina, fixing her eyes on her.

'How many times?' Mikko teased.

'Forget who you were. Be true to the part, to your characters' motivations and desires, because this is life and death.'

'You've given me the shivers,' said Bianca.

'Let's give it a go, take it step by step ... Kerstin, feel free to start whenever you're ready.'

'Thanks.'

The tall woman who had been hovering behind the others now moved forward on the stage, while those who weren't involved in the first scene took a step back.

Kerstin Tamm was in her fifties, with blue eyes, a strong jaw and acne scars on her cheeks. Her hair was tied back in two thin plaits.

Ramon leaned in to Mikko and whispered something in his ear. Mikko nodded impatiently.

'Focus, everyone,' Regina said without looking at them.

Kerstin lowered the script in her hand and began to recite the witches' spells with what sounded like a slight irony or scepticism to her voice.

'OK, let's keep going,' Regina said once she had finished.

Tommy took a step forward and cleared his throat. '*What bloody man is that?*' he asked.

Ramon started biting his nails. He looked deep in thought for a moment, then began to describe Macbeth's valour on the battlefield.

Regina largely left the actors to their own devices, but every now and again she stepped in to discuss the intentions behind a particular line or the political undercurrents in the text.

Forty-five minutes after they started, it was finally time for Bianca to put down her Coca-Cola and make her entry onto the stage. A heaviness settled over the room, as though it had followed her like some sort of train. Her impatient longing shone almost imperceptibly through the lines as she read the letter from her husband.

Mikko sauntered over to her on the stage with his fingers raised in a victory sign, but Regina immediately stopped him.

'Forget the past,' she said.

'Couldn't help myself,' he replied without glancing in her direction.

Julia had read some of the reviews of the last run, and she remembered that one of the critics had praised that gesture of youthful overconfidence. Clearly Regina wanted everyone to be completely reborn in their roles this time around.

Mikko's expressive face became solemn, an existential weariness in his pale blue eyes, as though the horrors of war were overshadowing the triumph in his heart from the very first greeting.

The scene between Macbeth and his wife quickly grew in intensity. The temperature seemed to rise, and they managed to convey the pent-up passion in their rapid exchange.

Bianca gripped Mikko's arm in an attempt to make him stay, and he turned sharply and gave her a shove. She lost her balance and tumbled backwards, causing her head to hit the floor with a dull thud.

'Christ,' Regina gasped, hurrying over.

'Shit, sorry,' said Mikko, bending down over her. 'Are you OK?'

Bianca sat up with a look of confusion on her face. 'Wow,' she mumbled, pressing a hand to the back of her head.

'What's wrong with you, Mikko?' Regina asked, getting down on her knees and examining Bianca's head. 'You're not bleeding, at least. Does it hurt?'

'It's OK,' she said, forcing herself up.

'Sorry, I just got carried away,' said Mikko, taking a few steps back.

'These things happen,' said Tommy.

'We'll have to bring in an intimacy coordinator,' Regina muttered with a sigh.

'Yeah, because some people just can't wrap their heads around this little thing called boundaries,' said Bianca.

'God, would you relax?' Mikko said with an irritated smile. 'I didn't *mean* to knock you over.'

'We'll have to take your word for that,' said Regina. 'But I must say, your aura is bright red right now, like—'

'My *aura?*'

'It's nervous, agg—'

'Oh, fuck off.'

'Nervous, aggressive and impulsive.'

'I don't know how anyone can be as woo-woo and brainwashed and woke as you and still expect people to take them seriously.'

'OK, Mikko, that's enough,' said Tommy. 'You don't have to agree with everything Regina says, but you know she's a bloody good director. Everyone does.'

'Shame no one thinks you're a good actor, though,' Mikko shot back, taking a step forward.

With a disappointed smile, Tommy held up a hand to keep Mikko at bay. 'Your moods really impact on everyone else, and—'

Mikko gripped his wrist and used his free hand to push Tommy's elbow back. Tommy instinctively leaned forward to lessen the pressure on his shoulder joint.

'Ow! Ow, stop!'

'Let go of him!' shouted Bianca.

'Kiss my arse,' Mikko snarled, forcing the older man down onto the floor.

'Stop,' Ramon growled.

Mikko turned to him with wide eyes and let go of Tommy.

'You'll be hearing from the health and safety officer, Mikko,' said Regina.

'Complete fucking madman,' Bianca muttered.

Mikko gestured aggressively, bringing his thumb and fingers together like a snapping beak, before turning and marching out of the room. Tommy got back onto his feet, and Regina suggested taking a thirty-minute break.

'Don't think too badly of us, will you?' Tommy said to Julia, massaging his shoulder. 'For the most part, we're all professionals, serious about what we do . . . I'm just sorry you're seeing us at our worst.'

Twenty

BIANCA'S FACE WAS PALE, AND she was unsteady on her feet as she headed off to the bathroom with a hand on the back of her head. Regina made her way back over to Julia at the production desk, Tommy was on the phone to someone, and Ramon sat down beside the prompter and wiped his mouth.

'Theatre is supposed to be physical, but not *this* physical,' Regina muttered.

'I understand,' Julia replied.

'Their chemistry was fucking great just before she fell over, though,' Ramon pointed out.

'Magical,' Julia agreed, noting that Tommy had left the room.

'It's so interesting, the way some people just *have* it,' Regina said with a nod. 'Don't get me wrong, people can work hard to achieve things, and I respect that ... but when it comes naturally to someone, that's something else. People like Ursula, like Bianca ... and Mikko, who never even went to drama school.'

'But Bianca only had a small part in the play last time, didn't she?' asked Julia.

'Ursula was originally playing Lady Macbeth,' Regina replied.

'Oh, I hadn't realised that,' said Julia, turning to Ursula. 'So you used to be an actor?'

'Yes. I shared a dressing room with Bianca. We helped each other with our lines.'

'Bianca really loves the theatre,' said Ramon.

'I know,' said Regina. 'I remember noticing her right away. She was always here, and she was hungry. Listening, observing, learning.'

'What happened?' asked Julia.

'We'd been working *so* hard,' Regina replied. 'The premiere was almost upon us, and we'd really nailed it, the whole thing was *hot* – right, Ramon?'

'I mean . . . I was pretty new to it all as well, but I remember thinking that I was in the part of a lifetime,' Ramon agreed, sniffing loudly.

'Everyone was at the very top of their game, but then Ursula had her accident. I mean, it was all just so unnecessary . . . Sorry, but that's how it felt,' Regina said with a smile.

'My own fault. It *was* stupid,' Ursula said quietly.

'How so?' asked Julia.

'I was in my dressing room, and I saw that my spinach juice had arrived, so I grabbed it and drank half before I realised it tasted much better than usual – like kiwi.'

'OK?'

'I have a pretty bad kiwi allergy,' Ursula continued with a gesture to her neck.

'Oof.'

'It felt like my throat was on fire, and I started coughing . . . Honestly, it all happened so fast. I only just managed to get up from the makeup chair before my airways completely closed up,' she continued, gesturing to herself again. 'I couldn't breathe, and I was all alone in the dressing room, so I panicked and grabbed a wire coat hanger, straightened it out and forced it down my throat so I could get some air ... It might have saved my life, but it also damaged my vocal cords and ...'

She shrugged and cleared her throat.

'The ambulance came, and we hit pause on everything, cancelled rehearsals,' Regina continued.

'It was just so stupid,' Ursula whispered.

'We knew pretty quickly that you were going to be OK, which was a huge relief,' said Regina. 'But what about the play? We tried to get the doctors to give us some sort of indication as to whether you'd be OK to continue, but they wouldn't ... so we knew it wasn't looking good.'

'We were all in shock,' said Ramon, fixing his dark eyes on her.

'It was total panic stations here,' Regina went on. 'The bosses wanted answers, said we couldn't postpone the premiere because Mikko was due on a film shoot as soon as we were done ... Bianca went to Helsinki to try to save her relationship with Nicolás, then came back for the crisis meeting. We had a vote, and the majority were in favour of giving her a shot, because she knew the part. Was it a risk? Absolutely. But what the hell were we supposed to do?'

'She was good, though,' said Ramon.

'Yes,' said Ursula, swallowing a painkiller dry.

'She showed what she was capable of, no doubt about it,' said Regina. 'It only took her a few days to have the lines nailed down ... but she didn't have time to really *inhabit* the part, that just wasn't possible.'

'Considering she found out about Nicolás's death at basically the same time, though … Jesus Christ, poor thing,' Ramon said admiringly. 'She gritted her teeth and made it through the premiere. I honestly didn't think she'd manage it.'

'Incredible,' Ursula said, her eyes lowered.

'But a week after that, the grief finally hit her and she collapsed on stage in front of a full house. And after that it was curtains for the rest of the run,' Ramon said with a sad smile as he checked his phone.

In her strange, soft voice, Ursula announced that she was going to get a coffee, and she made her way up onto the stage and over to the passage behind the black curtain.

'Speaking of Nicolás,' said Julia. 'What do you think happened to him?'

Regina slowly shook her head and pulled her file towards her.

'Some say it was an accident, others that it was suicide,' she said.

'There was a fight before he left for Helsinki,' said Julia, keen to keep the conversation going.

'Yes, Mikko was drunk and went too far,' Regina replied in an attempt to round things off.

'In what sense?'

'I don't know, I just remember seeing Bianca's bare breasts through the crowd in Riche,' said Regina. She sounded like she regretted saying anything.

'She was wearing a blouse with press studs down the front, and Mikko came up with the genius idea of tearing it open so he could lick wine off her tits,' Ramon explained.

'Yikes,' Julia whispered.

128

'Don't get me wrong, Bianca was drunk too,' Ramon continued. 'She tried to button it up again, but Nicolás barged over to Mikko and punched him in the face. Mikko dropped like a rock, Bianca started screaming, and Nicolás grabbed Mikko's hair, like this, and clenched his fist ... Mikko was totally pathetic, saying, "Please, not my nose, I'm an actor ... " Nicolás didn't have time to actually hit him again, someone pulled them apart and he wound up being thrown out. Then Bianca ran off after him, and that was that.'

With a frown, Regina had started scribbling in the margin of her script. It was clear that she didn't want to talk about that evening. Either that, or she really needed to get on with her work.

Kerstin had a backache, and was lying down on the stage floor with her knees pulled into her chest, rocking slowly from side to side.

Ramon got to his feet and wandered up onto the stage, checked his phone again and then left the room. He had dark sweat patches beneath both arms, Julia noticed as she grabbed her cane and moved over to the edge of the stage, where she sat down and gazed out at the black and green rooftops through one of the small windows.

She made a mental note to search the archive for more information about Ursula's accident before her thoughts drifted to Mikko's sexual harassment of Bianca.

What did the incident at the bar really mean? Was it as simple as it looked – an aggressive violation of Bianca's integrity, an attempt to humiliate her – or had there been some sort of secret attraction between them at the time? Or could it simply be down to a drunken lack of boundaries?

As in so many countries, the #MeToo movement had swept through Sweden like some sort of indiscriminate, purifying wave, and Julia was starting to understand why it had never gone any further than anonymous testimony about unnamed perpetrators within the world of theatre.

'Oh, sweetie,' Regina shouted, getting to her feet.

Bianca had come back into the room with a bottle of water and a tub of salad.

'How are you feeling?' the director asked as she made her way down from the stage.

'I'm not sure. A bit weird, but I took a painkiller. Probably just need something to eat,' Bianca said as she passed the production table.

Julia took out her phone and saw that she had two messages from Sid. In the first, he had written that he was sorry for rushing off yesterday, but that he hoped she'd had a good swim. Two hours after that, he had written to say that he was free to swing by Bianca's place and install the security cameras after work today.

Twenty-One

Bianca gazed out of the window as she slowly ate her salad with a little wooden fork. Tommy came back into the room with a banana in his hand, walked over to Regina's desk and pretended to plug it into her phone charger.

Kerstin came across the stage and sat down beside Julia with a sigh. She was so tall that her feet reached the floor.

'Back trouble?' asked Julia.

'Mmm, need to see my chiropractor.'

Her denim jacket was tight over her shoulders and chest, her greying plaits hanging limply beside her scarred cheeks.

'I've been thinking about the fact that Bianca stepped up to take on the role of Lady Macbeth after Ursula's allergic reaction. What happened to her lines?' asked Julia.

'Kerstin took them,' Bianca replied, turning towards them. 'I see.'

'And she was great,' Regina said as she peeled the banana.

'I had ... what, two days to prepare? And I knew I needed to quickly find a way in,' said Kerstin. 'So I pretended I was Stellan Skarsgård playing a witch.'

'You never told me that,' Regina said with a laugh.

'Of course not.'

'Stellan would've been great as a witch,' said Tommy.

'Don't tell me you've worked with him too?' asked Bianca.

'No,' he replied. 'But my dad was a teacher at the Olympia School in Helsingborg. Stellan was one of his pupils there, and they travelled around the county doing talks about ... drugs, I think it was.'

'Can't have been contraception, in any case,' Kerstin joked.

'No,' he laughed.

Bianca tossed her food container into the bin once she finished her salad, then asked Regina if it was OK if she took the rest of the day off.

'Absolutely. Good idea, you do that, and I'll give you a ring later,' the director replied, stroking her arm.

'I'll head off too, in that case,' said Julia, reaching for her cane.

'Will you be joining us again tomorrow?' asked Regina.

'I'd love to, if that's OK?'

Julia followed Bianca through the room and out into the corridor, past rehearsal room two.

'Sidney said he could come over to fit some security cameras at your place later, if you want them,' she said.

'What do you think? Isn't that a bit over the top?'

'I'd recommend having them installed, mostly so you can feel a bit safer,' Julia explained. 'You'll have an app on your phone, meaning you can check no one has broken in while you're out or in the shower.'

'God, now you're really scaring me,' said Bianca, pulling a terrified face.

'No, I just mean ... Look, you already have new locks, so no one is getting in. But I don't want you to have to worry at all,' Julia continued as they got into the lift.

'Right,' said Bianca, though she didn't sound convinced.

'I'm serious.'

'OK, then,' she said with a smile, holding her pass up to the reader and pressing the button.

The two women stood in silence as the doors closed and the machinery started to whir.

'Things seem pretty tense between Tommy and Regina,' said Julia.

'Are you thinking about anything in particular?'

'No, just a few different things. The first day, in the cafeteria, for example. She got up and left as soon as Tommy came over.'

'I don't think—'

'And she wasn't exactly nice when she mentioned that he'd been Ingmar Bergman's punching bag and ended up in psychiatric care.'

'No, I know.'

'And she told me she spat in his face when you—'

'That's true, you're right.' Bianca cut her off, holding her hands up. 'I guess I'd just stopped noticing ... They only got divorced a few months before we started rehearsals last time.'

They left the lift and started walking down a corridor that immediately made Julia think of the rehab centre. The doors separating the various sections were all white, with brown trim around the windows.

'And they'd been struggling for a long time before that,' Bianca continued. 'They'd tried therapy and everything, but some betrayals are just too big to be able to talk your way through.'

'I suppose so,' Julia mumbled.

The pools of light from the overhead bulbs were like scattered puddles on the bluish-grey vinyl floor.

A crumpled sheet of paper with the word 'Toilet' scribbled on it had been taped onto a narrow door.

'Their issues stem from the fact that they've got an adult daughter who lives on the street,' Bianca said quietly, glancing at Julia with watery eyes.

'Surely there's something they can do about that?'

'I don't know. I think she has autism, or maybe it's called ASD these days. It's not something they ever talk about, but I know Regina is mad with Tommy because he just let their daughter go, gave up on her, acting like she doesn't even exist . . .'

'What does Tommy have to say?'

'He's too nice to get into a fight with Regina,' Bianca replied as she came to a halt. 'He just nods whenever she has a go at him . . . And drinks far too much, but plenty of people do that.'

'And what about Regina? Who is she?'

'She's like a mum to me, but she's also incredibly wishy-washy, on a personal level . . . but that's all down to trust, if you ask me. All that stuff disappears once she's in director mode. It's like she gets a laser focus then. If you go over to her place, though . . . there are crystals everywhere, in glasses and pans, dotted around the bed. She earths herself on some weird rubber mattress with a cable going out of the door and into the ground. She's got some kind of water swirling device fitted to her pipes, a portrait of Sai Baba on the wall, and she meditates and eats according to her blood group or her horoscope, or in line with ayurvedic principles . . .'

On the wall outside dressing room 7303, there was a small rectangle of plexiglass with the names *Bianca Salo* and *Stina Stiernstedt* written in black text.

Bianca reached into her bag for her key, but the door was already ajar.

'You really do need to keep this locked,' said Julia.

'I know. I did talk to Stina about it, but she's a bit forgetful. You're probably thinking I'm one to talk, but she's worse than me.'

Bianca knocked, and when there was no reply she showed Julia inside. The dark room was cluttered, with two sofas, a lambskin armchair, two reading lamps with white fabric shades, a plug-in radiator and a round coffee table full of fan mail and letters from autograph hunters.

'I'm sorry to bring this up . . .' said Julia, using her cane to poke at the letters. 'But someone saw Mikko coming out of your dressing room on Thursday.'

'In the evening?' Bianca gasped.

'I don't have an exact time, I just need to know what he was doing here.'

'No idea.'

'They saw him shove a pair of knickers into his pocket.'

'Aha, I bet he did,' Bianca said with a grin. 'He's decided he wants to sleep with Stina. I tried to warn her, but she's funny, she just says that she's planning to let him knock her up. She knows she needs to play hard to get if she wants to keep him interested, to say no and blush if he asks for her knickers.'

Towards the back of the cramped dressing room, which had a sloping ceiling and a small window behind a brownish-grey curtain, there was a white table with two chairs and two makeup mirrors.

Bianca walked over to the table and put her bag down, and for a split second Julia saw her face reflected from three angles, like three different people.

The actress opened the drawer under the table, lifted up a pair of old slippers in a plastic bag and reached beneath for a silver pouch. From that, she produced a small, pale blue ashtray, a metal Zippo lighter and a crumpled pack of cigarettes.

Bianca then kneeled on one of the sofas, opened the window and leaned out. 'The whole building is no smoking,' she explained with a smirk.

She used her lips to pull a cigarette out of the pack, flicked back the cover on the lighter and used her thumb to turn the little wheel. An enormous flame flared upwards, filling the room with light. Bianca shrieked and scrambled back, waving her hand above her head. The lighter clattered to the floor. The curtain had caught fire, but Julia moved forward and used her cane to pull it down so that she could stamp out the flames.

'What the hell?!' Bianca panted, staring at herself in the mirror.

'Did you burn yourself?'

'Just singed my hair a bit, but . . . what the hell just happened?'

'I think someone might have tampered with your lighter,' Julia replied. 'I'll take it away with me and have a closer look at it.'

She tore out a sheet of paper from her notepad, steadied herself against the sofa with her free hand and bent down. She then put the sheet of paper on the floor and used a pen to push the lighter on top.

'I don't know ...' said Bianca. 'It feels kind of lame to turn up the flame on someone's lighter, if you see what I mean.'

'It could have been much worse. It could have hit you in the eye. For all we know, it might have been supposed to explode. I'm taking this extremely seriously.'

Julia folded the sheet of paper around the lighter, taking care not to touch it, then carefully transferred the small parcel into her bag.

'OK,' Bianca whispered.

'Who else knows about your secret smoking habit?'

'No one ... Or ... It's not like I'm super secretive about it.'

'When did you last use the lighter?' asked Julia.

'It must've been yesterday, after the read-through ... No, that's not right. I had half a cigarette earlier today, right before the rehearsal.'

Twenty-Two

S ID WAS WAITING OUTSIDE THE door to Bianca's building in Nytorget when she and Julia got out of the taxi. His dark hair was getting long, lending his face a new softness. He was wearing a pair of black combat trousers and a black sweater with leather patches on the elbows, and on the pavement in front of him, there were two sturdy green canvas bags.

'This is Sidney Mendelson,' said Julia.

'Hi,' he replied, holding out a hand to Bianca.

'Bianca,' she said with a smile, gripping his hand.

'I saw your last performance in *The Seagull*. You were incredible as Nina.'

'Do you think so?'

'My eyes were welling up towards the end.'

Bianca laughed happily and let them into the building, then led them over to the lift.

'It was incredibly powerful,' Julia agreed.

'Thank you.'

The doors rattled shut, and the lift slowly started moving upwards, the machinery clanking loudly.

Julia studied herself in the mirror. The scar on her cheek looked pale pink in the strange lighting.

Sid had just started to say something about the security cameras when Bianca put a hand on his arm.

'I know I'm probably a bit of a narcissist,' she said with a smile. 'But being filmed around the clock still feels a bit much, even for me.'

'You'll be the only one with access to the feeds,' Sid replied.

'Not you?'

'No, it's—'

'Ah, that's a shame,' she joked.

Julia felt butterflies in her stomach as the lift started to slow. She lost contact with the floor and floated weightlessly in the cramped space.

Sid laughed briefly, then his face turned serious.

The machinery stopped clanking.

The lift came to a complete standstill, swaying slightly as it hovered in the shaft.

Julia saw that Sid's cheeks had flushed a little, just beneath his eyes.

A slight smile was playing on Bianca's lips, and she slowly reached up and pushed a lock of blonde hair back behind her ear without taking her eyes off him.

The movement dispersed a waft of singed hair through the cramped space.

Sid looked away, and his wide pupils slowly contracted, his pulse returning to normal.

Julia instinctively found herself thinking that as long as the two of them didn't spend any more time together in lifts, nothing would happen.

Bianca licked her lips and tried to catch Sid's eye in the mirror, but he turned his head and looked straight at Julia.

She saw the emergency lighting come on in the aisle, oxygen masks dangling from the compartments above the seats.

Julia sighed as she felt gravity take hold of her again, and the lift continued upwards to the fourth floor.

'In all seriousness,' said Sid. 'It's great that we could sort these out for you so quickly.'

'They'll cope without me at the theatre,' Bianca said breezily as she unlocked the door.

'Bianca had a bit of an accident earlier,' Julia explained.

'Ah, it was nothing.'

The actress made Sid a double espresso, then he took her around the apartment and showed her where he thought the cameras should go. Julia helped herself to a glass of water and sat down at the kitchen table with her cane against the radiator. She took out her phone, opened the news archive and searched back to the period before the last *Macbeth* premiere. It didn't take her long to find an article in *Expressen*.

BREAKING
ACTRESS URSULA ANDERSSON HOSPITALISED

The emergency services were called to the Royal Dramatic Theatre this evening following reports of someone with life-threatening breathing difficulties. Director Regina Muhammed found Ursula Andersson on the floor outside her dressing room and dialled 112.

The actress was taken by ambulance to the Karolinska Hospital, and is reported to be in a serious but stable condition.

The premiere of Shakespeare's tragedy Macbeth is slated to take place in three days' time, with Ursula Andersson playing the female lead opposite Mikko Järvinen. A spokesperson for Dramaten said that it was too soon for any updates on the actress's condition, or on whether the premiere will be postponed.

Julia kept searching, but the only direct follow-up she could find was a mini interview with Ursula from *Dagens Nyheter* a week later, in which she explained that she had suffered a serious allergic reaction after drinking a juice containing kiwi. Aside from that, there were only a few brief mentions of the incident in the negative reviews of the production, and in the articles published after Bianca's breakdown on stage.

It was almost incomprehensible that Bianca had ever agreed to take on the part of Lady Macbeth so soon after Nicolás's death, thought Julia.

Still, given the lack of information from his family, perhaps she had simply struggled to take it in. Bianca had been living with him for three years, after all, but had received nothing but a terse, formal email about his sudden death.

It must have felt completely surreal.

And when the letter from him later arrived, she was so broken that she hadn't been able to bring herself to open it.

But Julia needed to read it.

Bianca was probably afraid that it would lay the blame at her feet or something equally awful.

Julia found herself thinking about how much Bianca had probably dwelled on everything afterwards. The situation at Riche, the fight, her hurried journey home from Helsinki in order to make it to the crisis meeting at the theatre.

Everything that had led up to her collapse on stage.

Julia heard her giggling flirtatiously at something Sid had said, and she put down her phone, sipped her water and looked out at the pale sky on the other side of the window.

Twenty-Three

THE VARNISHED FLOORBOARDS CREAKED UNDER-
FOOT as Sid walked across the living room. Julia
turned her head towards the doorway, and a moment
later he and Bianca came into the kitchen.

Sid put his cup down on the counter and pointed out a
suitable spot for the final camera. Bianca replied that she trusted
his judgement fully by this point.

'Why don't you get started in the hallway,' Julia told Sid.
'And we'll wait in here.'

'I might make a bit of noise,' he said, closing the door behind
him as he left the kitchen.

Bianca put a pot of water to heat on the stove, then sat down
opposite Julia. Her face was animated, her shapely lips curling
into an eager smile. 'I think I'm starting to understand why
you've been having such a hard time letting go,' she said.

'But I have to,' Julia mumbled in reply.

'Do you really—'

The loud whirr of the drill cut her off. It only lasted around
fifteen seconds, but the sudden silence afterwards felt silky smooth.

'I know I have to accept that what he and I had is gone for
good,' said Julia.

'But you still want him in your life.'

'Yes, he . . . I need him in it, there's no other way.'

Bianca got up and took the pan off the heat, then poured the hot water into a teapot and set down two large cups on the table.

'You only have one heart,' she said.

'Speaking of which, I went to see Sonny.'

'In paradise?'

'Yes.'

'What did you think?' Bianca asked as she took a seat.

'I don't think he's your stalker.'

'No.'

'But he also doesn't seem to understand how you could have left him.'

'Because he's such a fantastic lover,' said Bianca.

'Is he?'

'No.' She laughed and poured tea into the two cups.

'Sonny seems to live a pretty laid-back life, surrounded by women . . .'

'Who've all lost their clothes.' Bianca nodded.

'Is that what it was like when you and Nicolás lived there?' asked Julia.

'We didn't have orgies or anything like that, but broadly, yeah. Showering outside, sleeping together . . .'

'It's just that you mentioned that Nicolás was a Catholic, and—'

'He became much more religious after he became a diplomat.'

'Was that why he attacked Mikko in the bar?'

A series of red blotches had flared up on Bianca's cheeks. She wrapped her hands around the cup in front of her and met Julia's eye.

'There's a natural physicality between actors on stage, during rehearsals,' she explained. 'And that's absolutely crucial. But often ... often that physicality tips over into something else. I don't know how to explain it ... It's almost seen as inevitable in the world of theatre ... and the majority of us women have learnt to accept it, tried to deal with it, while certain men have exploited it ... And sometimes it goes too far.'

'Is that what happened that night at Riche?'

Bianca blew on her tea and took a hesitant sip. 'Mikko kept going on and on about being able to see my nipples through my blouse. He said they got hard after he pointed it out and that he wanted to pour wine over me, etcetera etcetera ... I told him to calm down, to shut up and leave me alone. I was drunk too, so I don't know if I laughed or smiled as I said it, but it ended with him tearing my blouse open, right in front of everyone ... And Nicolás just lost it.'

'How did that make you feel?' Julia asked quietly.

Bianca shook her head, and her big eyes welled up. 'I was ashamed. Of myself, of my behaviour, of having been exposed like that. I was embarrassed by how aggressive Nicolás had been, too ... Though at the same time, I thought Mikko probably deserved being taken down a peg or two – or three ... But on the other hand, I don't need a man to defend my honour. I'm not a fucking trophy, you know? I'm a person. I went back to Nicolás's place, and we had a huge fight. It was horrible. And then I felt like I had to go to Helsinki with him, to try to straighten everything out, because he was still mad at me.'

Sid turned on the vacuum cleaner in the hallway.

'Did it work?'

'We stayed up talking half the night. I don't know how many times I swore that I wasn't cheating on him, that I never had and never would ... And then we had sex, went to sleep and had breakfast in bed before I left to come back to Stockholm. I thought I'd saved our relationship.'

Bianca trailed off and dried the tears from her cheeks.

'We still don't know why he died,' Julia said softly.

'No. But since then, I've thought a lot ...'

The muffled sound of an electric screwdriver reached them through the kitchen door.

'Thought about what?'

'I can't do this,' Bianca whispered, taking another sip of tea.

'You have the letter from him in your safe,' said Julia.

'Please ...'

'I'd really like to read it.'

'But it's private,' Bianca replied, lowering her cup to the table. 'I feel bad enough as it is. I don't need to know what he was accusing me of.'

'You don't have to read it yourself.'

'I hear what you're saying, but the answer is still no. That's a door I really don't want to open. Not right now, anyway.'

Julia studied the actress's furrowed brow and thoughtful gaze. It was clear she was thinking deeply about something. Something she wasn't sure she wanted to share.

'Jealousy can be difficult to deal with, because it doesn't follow any kind of logic,' Julia began in an attempt to lure Bianca back into the conversation.

'I don't know,' she sighed. 'I understand that what happened was hard for Nicolás ... With Mikko, I mean.'

'In what sense?'

Bianca cleared her throat, an uneasy look on her face. 'Nicolás knew about something that happened when I was single, before I met him. I told him about it early on, because I didn't want to have any secrets from him.'

'What happened?'

'I want to start by saying that ... it's like a kind of compulsion for Mikko. He finds girls who are interested in the theatre, talented girls, and he exploits their dreams, his fame, his position of power, to get them to have sex with him, even though none of them really want it.'

'It seems like you've given a lot of thought to this?'

'Yeah, I have,' Bianca said with a weary smile.

'Are you in therapy?'

'I was for two years.'

There was a high-pitched whirring sound as Sid drilled into one of the walls, and they heard the plaster dust hitting the floor.

'Go on,' said Julia.

'OK, so I was in the last term of drama school, and Mikko came to see our final show. During the after-party, he started piling on the praise. I was already pretty drunk by that point, but he told me he was going to be in *The Wild Duck* at Dramaten and that he thought he'd be able to get me a small part.'

'If it sounds too good to be true ...' Julia said with a nod.

Bianca closed her eyes and tipped her head back for a moment. 'I try not to feel ashamed about any of this, because I was young and being used. Maybe it was naive, but it taught me something about life ...'

'What happened?'

Bianca took a deep breath and then looked straight at Julia without even a hint of a smile. 'I don't actually remember everything he said, but it basically boiled down to him needing to be sure he could trust me, that we understood each other ... So I went to the bathroom with him, and we had sex.'

'I understand,' said Julia, brushing the scar on her cheek with her fingertips.

'It wasn't really that bad, though I can see now that he was using me.'

'Yes.'

'He'd already left the party by the time I came back out of the bathroom. I didn't have his number, so I just went home, took a shower, cried for a bit and then fell asleep,' she said. 'But then we bumped into each other at a bar a few weeks later, and I played it up, telling him that, basically, it had been great for me, exactly what I needed ... acting like I thought we'd entered into some sort of consensual sexual relationship. And, you know, I just kept talking like I was expecting the part he'd mentioned ... We had sex two more times, at my place, and suddenly I had a foot in the door at Dramaten.'

Bianca used her hands to cover her face.

'You got him to keep his word,' said Julia.

'I know you'll probably think this sounds a bit cynical, but from my point of view, for me ... it was my way of trying to cope with the fact that I'd been used. Like I was turning the situation on its head. I didn't want to be a victim. I wanted something good to come out of what I'd been through.'

'And after that?'

'No sex in the champagne room. I kept working at Dramaten, met Nicolás and told Mikko that I really wanted to give that relationship a try – which he respected, or so he said. Though he didn't.'

Twenty-Four

BEFORE SID HURRIED BACK TO work, he connected the motion-activated cameras to Bianca's Wi-Fi network, and helped her to download the app and to create an account with a strong password. He then showed her how to view each of the rooms in real time and to access the footage saved in the cloud.

'It's not over for him, either,' Bianca said once he had gone.

'Yes, it is.'

'His eyes tell a different story.'

The actress had just started to clear the table when there was a knock at the door.

'That must be Regina,' she said, heading through to the hallway.

'Wait,' Julia shouted, grabbing her cane and setting off after her.

Bianca turned around, one hand already on the handle. 'What?'

Julia raised an eyebrow.

'Right,' said Bianca. 'Check the peephole first.' She leaned towards the door.

'You should really have the personal alarm in your hand, too,' said Julia.

'I know.'

There was a metallic click as she turned the lock, then she cracked the door open – the guard still in place – and waved to Regina through the narrow gap. Bianca closed the door, checked the peephole again, released the guard and opened it fully.

'What are you doing?' Regina asked as she came in.

'Can't be too careful as far as you're concerned,' Bianca replied.

'Quite right.'

Regina kicked off her shoes. Her grey plait was messy, and she was wearing a black vintage suit and a white blouse with a yellowed collar.

'How's the head?' she asked.

'Haven't had any complaints so far,' Bianca replied with a wink.

'Ha.' The director smiled and started making her way through to the lounge.

'How did the rest of the rehearsal go?' Bianca asked.

'Mikko was late coming back, but he pulled himself together – he always does when he's feeling guilty . . . Tommy's really starting to dig deep, too, working methodically. Ramon had some sort of idea about him being a spider and . . . Ursula read your lines, which gave the whole thing a weird feel.'

'Was Mikko the only one who was late?' asked Julia.

'Yes.'

'How late?'

'Fifteen minutes.'

They slumped down onto the deep sofa, and Julia moved around to the other side of the low coffee table so that she could observe their interactions.

'I totally remember Ursula from rehearsals last time,' said Bianca. 'She was insanely good. I didn't want to admit it at the time, but her Lady was so much better than mine.'

'Given the short amount of time you had, you were incredible,' said Regina, stroking her arm.

'You don't have to say that,' said Bianca, though she smiled with satisfaction.

Julia stood with her back to the bookcase, leaning against her cane, and saw Bianca point up at the camera on the ceiling.

'So you're on film twenty-four seven now, huh?' said Regina.

'Yeah, it's hard work keeping my belly sucked in all the time.'

'Seriously, though ... I've never really understood the whole cameras-at-home thing.'

'I've got an app,' said Bianca, holding up her phone for Regina. 'See? We look like little dolls.'

'God, we're so cute,' Regina said, waving for the camera.

'I know.'

'Can you zoom in so you can see our faces?'

'Yeah, but look, the resolution isn't great,' Bianca explained as she demonstrated it.

'The cameras are really only so that Bianca knows it's safe to come into the apartment,' said Julia.

'Of course, I'm just curious,' said Regina, tucking one of the cushions behind her back. 'But aren't you going to end up with hours and hours of footage to check before you come in?'

'The cameras are motion activated, which means the footage is only saved if there's someone in the apartment,' Julia replied.

'Can you trick them by moving incredibly slowly?'

'God, what a creepy question,' Bianca said with a gasp.

Regina laughed and leaned back, fiddling with the piece of rose quartz hanging on a leather cord around her neck.

Bianca got up, smoothed her trousers and went through to the kitchen. Regina watched her go, then turned to Julia, who was still standing by the bookcase.

'Are you going to find her stalker?' she asked. 'Or is it just that Bianca has got a bit too into character?'

'Oh, she definitely has a stalker,' Julia replied.

'But not Nicolás?'

'We'll see.'

Regina frowned and smiled, unsure whether or not to take Julia's response as a joke.

'What makes things slightly tricky is that we constantly need to be thinking about Bianca's safety, even though that's not strictly our job,' Julia continued. 'That's why we've been helping her with the cameras and the alarm. In an ideal world, she wouldn't be alone at any point.'

Bianca came back into the room carrying three glasses, a carafe of water and some sliced lime on a tray.

'I can sleep over here tonight, if you like,' Regina told her. 'We could get a takeaway.'

'I can't this evening,' Bianca replied, pouring water for each of them.

'OK?'

'Ramon and I are dating,' the actress continued without looking up.

'Wow ... I ... I don't know what to say,' Regina replied, tugging gently on her plait.

'It's nothing serious,' Bianca added.

'No, OK.' Regina cleared her throat.

'But a girls' evening tomorrow would be great.'

'I'll check, but I'm not sure tomorrow works for me.'

'It would be so nice – you could read my fortune again.'

Regina got up, said goodbye to Julia and then headed out into the hall. Bianca followed her, laughing anxiously at something the director said and likely forgetting to check the peephole before unlocking the door.

Regina hadn't been able to hide her disappointment, thought Julia. She might even have wanted Bianca to notice it.

Julia heard the door close, the lock click, and then Bianca came back into the room.

'Ramon said you'd already worked out that we were together,' she said as she sat down in the armchair.

'The very first time you mentioned him.'

'Seriously?'

'Yes. What did you make of Regina's reaction just now?'

Bianca smiled apologetically. 'She really cares, always has, and I love her for that. But she's ... a bit possessive, is that the word?'

'Mmm.'

'It's like she forgets I'm not actually her daughter sometimes, and she doesn't think anyone is good enough for me.'

'Like Ramon?'

'Like Ramon, like Nicolás ...'

'What do you like about Ramon?' asked Julia.

'Is this where I'm meant to blush?'

'So it's purely physical?'

Bianca raised an eyebrow. 'Isn't everything?' she replied with a grin.

'No, but a lot of things are.'

'He makes me happy, gives me butterflies. He's really romantic, too. He's actually taking me out to dinner this evening.'

'Where are you going?'

'A restaurant called Två små svin, over—'

'In Årsta.' Julia cut her off.

'Yeah, that's where he lives.'

'What time?'

'Seven. Why, are you going to tag along?'

'I'll be there for a while, just to check whether anyone is spying on you.'

'Other than you, you mean?'

Twenty-Five

JULIA AND SID HAD PULLED up to the kerb next to the bus stop outside the Danish restaurant on Årstavägen.

She was in the passenger seat, watching people walk by along the pavement. Through the tinted side window, Sid took pictures of everyone who entered Två små svin, paused for a little too long outside or displayed even the slightest odd behaviour.

On the other side of the fogged-up window of the restaurant, Julia could see Ramon and Bianca. They were eating elaborate open sandwiches and drinking beer and schnapps, chatting and laughing and holding hands across the table.

'Does this mean we're officially working together again?' she asked, glancing over to Sid.

'I don't know, I haven't really thought about it ... Do you want to?'

She attempted an indifferent shrug and swallowed hard. 'If you want,' she said.

'Only if you need my help.'

'You know I work better when you're around. Everything is better when you're around,' she replied, pressing her lips firmly together in an effort to stop herself from crying.

Sid allowed her heartfelt words to pass without comment and said that work was pretty quiet at the moment, so it looked like he would be able to take some time off if necessary.

He then raised his camera and took a few pictures of a man moving impatiently up the rocky slope beside the restaurant.

'You drifted off on me in the lift,' he said.

'It's not something I can control,' she replied, fiddling with the handle of her cane.

'You say that, but have you tried—'

'I can't help it, but OK. I'm sorry if it made you uncomfortable.'

'It didn't, I just wanted to say that I noticed.'

'I noticed a few things, too,' she blurted out.

'Like what?'

'Like Bianca's flirtatiousness . . . I don't think it's anything to do with a need to seduce people, more her own survival.'

'What do you mean?'

'If a woman is beautiful and successful, like Bianca is, she constantly needs to let everyone else know that she sees them. She has to acknowledge and flatter them.'

'I guess.'

A bus was approaching from behind, and Sid had to move out of its way. He did a loop of the roundabout and then pulled back up in the same spot.

As they watched the restaurant, Julia told him about Mikko using his position to have sex with Bianca before she had even graduated from drama school, and how she had then turned that on its head and used him too, in order to escape her feelings of humiliation.

Sid got out and walked down the street to Jettz Burger, returning with a couple of cheeseburgers, some fries and two Coca-Colas.

Julia continued where she had left off, telling him all about Bianca's life and her first few years at Dramaten, when she was employed on a project-by-project basis and played various minor parts. She explained that the actress had met Nicolás at a festival in Oslo, and that the two had spent almost a year living with her ex-boyfriend Sonny and his friends on a farm in Roslagen, growing their own food and smoking weed. That Nicolás had then got a job with the Brazilian embassy, and they had both moved back to Stockholm.

Julia then moved on to Regina, telling Sid that she had been given the honour of directing *Macbeth* by the previous artistic director of the theatre, and that she had managed to cast both Mikko and Ursula Andersson in the lead roles.

'Bianca was originally supposed to play a punky witch,' she said as she finished the last mouthful of her burger.

She wiped her hands on a napkin before she continued, repeating what Regina and Ursula had said about Bianca's strengths: that she had got to know everyone at the theatre from the very beginning, showing an interest in everything, proofreading for the playwrights and chatting to the lighting engineers and stage techs, attending every rehearsal and learning all of the parts by heart.

'She shared a dressing room with Ursula and helped her learn her lines,' Julia went on. 'And she followed Regina's improv work and deeper analyses.'

'What, and then her luck changed?' asked Sid, helping himself to Julia's leftover fries.

'Yes, after Ursula had a bad reaction to some juice. Her throat closed up, and she was rushed to hospital in an ambulance.'

Julia recapped Bianca's version of what happened at Riche, when Mikko tore open her blouse and Nicolás got jealous.

'I asked Ramon about it, and he made it sound like Mikko getting punched and humiliated in front of everyone was funny ... But for Bianca, the whole thing was a horrible experience. I mean, she had her breasts exposed, and her fiancé punched a famous actor. She dragged Nicolás home and ended up going to Helsinki with him the next day, in an attempt to save their relationship. The day after that, she flew back to Stockholm on her own for a crisis meeting at the theatre, agreed to take on Ursula's part, and spent the next few days rehearsing ahead of the premiere – despite having just found out that Nicolás was dead. And a week later, she broke down on stage.'

'*Gam zu l'tova.*'

An older man knocked on the window of the restaurant, trying to get Bianca's attention, then sang a few lines from 'O sole mio' with both hands pressed to his chest. Bianca flashed him a smile, blew him a couple of kisses and then continued her conversation with Ramon.

'Nice,' said Sid.

Julia rounded off by telling him about what happened during their rehearsal recently, with Mikko shoving Bianca so hard that she fell and hit her head, and someone tampering with her lighter at some point between ten and twelve that same morning.

'More fire,' said Sid.

'Yup.'

'You should have the lighter analysed.'

160

'I've got it in my bag. I haven't touched it.'

'Good.'

'It's clear to me that Bianca does have a stalker,' said Julia. 'Someone whose obsession with her has started to tip over into aggression . . . I need to try to find out how many people were near her dressing room both when her dress caught fire and when the lighter was tampered with.'

'That should really narrow things down.'

'But at the same time, we don't even know if Nicolás is really dead. That's just what his family said.'

'I'll look into it.'

An old woman carrying a sheet of cardboard reading 'Jesus Loves You' went into the restaurant and held up her message to the diners.

'I always say that my dad was an atheist, but he wasn't, not really,' said Sid. 'He used to argue that no one knows more about God than anyone else – whether they're a sect leader, a rabbi or a priest . . . and that if they claim they do, they're lying. That's the simple truth. There are a lot of people who are very knowledgeable about the various religious texts, of course, but the people who actually wrote those texts didn't know any more about God than anyone else.'

The woman re-emerged from the restaurant and walked straight towards their car, holding up her sign for Sid to see. He raised a thumb to her, and she went on her way with a smile.

'But there's a difference between knowing and believing,' said Julia.

'Not according to my dad there isn't. He would argue that you can't even *believe* in God, because there's absolutely nothing to prove his existence . . . You can look at a bridge over a river, study it and then say you believe it'll work as a crossing, but if there isn't a bridge – no planks, no ropes, nothing – then you can't believe it'll work.'

'OK, Sid . . . but I believe in crystals,' she teased him.

After two hours, Bianca and Ramon finally emerged from the restaurant. He had his arm around her waist beneath her open coat, and they seemed a little unsteady on their feet, briefly stopping to kiss.

Julia finished off the last of her Coca-Cola.

Bianca said something to Ramon with a big smile, wiped a little of her lipstick from his mouth and kissed him again, then they started walking.

A group of excited young men were filming them on their phones.

Let's head back home now, Julia wanted to say. To our place on Roslagsgatan, our wonderful apartment. We can make some tea and sandwiches, pretend it's the weekend. Light the shabbat candles and recite the Kiddush together. We can sip our wine. It's all still there: the apartment hasn't been sold, our marriage hasn't fallen apart, we still trust each other. Everything is as it should be, everything is good between us again.

Sid gathered up the leftovers in the paper bag, got out of the car and threw them into a bin, then sat back down behind the wheel, started the engine and pulled away from the kerb.

Twenty-Six

THEY HAD NOW BEEN SITTING in the dark car outside the low white house at Svärdlångsvägen 13 for forty-five minutes. There was no sign of anyone out and about, though the lights were still on in some of the windows nearby, the flickering glow of a TV dancing across a trellis.

Every now and again, a car drove by on the main road.

Through the windscreen and the sparse bushes, Julia and Sid could see almost straight into two of Ramon's windows around thirty metres away.

From what they knew so far, everything pointed to Bianca's stalker having entered a particularly active phase, a dangerous period in which he was likely to seek out physical contact with her in order to sate his urges. A period in which his longing for power became increasingly frustrated.

Sid got out and mounted a digital camera on the roof of the car, then sat back down behind the wheel, took out an iPad and turned the camera towards the house.

The pale light made the image look black and white: the plastered facade, the grass, the bushes and trees, the white plastic furniture in the garden, the barbecue.

Julia reached for the tablet and tried zooming in on the rainwater barrel beneath the drainpipe before panning over the wall to the dark kitchen and bedroom window.

The soft glow from an indirect source of light illuminated the bed, which was cluttered with black decorative cushions.

On the football pitch on the other side of the road, the last few shouts petered out as Julia tried to describe the various figures around Bianca to Sid.

'Regina loves her, possibly a bit too much . . . She wants her to, and I quote, "be the daughter she wishes she'd had",' Julia said as she scanned the area again. 'And as for Mikko . . . he comes across as a self-obsessed misogynist, like so many men. It's possible he felt duped by Bianca once he realised she had never actually been attracted to him.'

'And then her fiancé punched and humiliated him,' Sid pointed out.

'Punched, yes, but humiliated is up for debate. He was afraid of getting his face messed up, which is a natural reaction.'

'But it doesn't fit with his self-image.'

'No, that's true.'

Julia turned the camera towards the window again and saw a grey figure in Ramon's kitchen. It was Bianca, lighting a cigarette beneath the extractor fan as she talked to someone out of view.

'What about Tommy?' asked Sid.

'Tommy doesn't have an alibi for the time when the dress caught fire. He comes across as kind, conflict-averse . . . possibly even a little boring. A hard-working actor with a permanent ensemble position at the theatre. But Regina can't stand him and seems to blame all their daughter's problems on him.'

164

'And Ramon?'

'Ramon has something restless about him, a kind of imbalance. He's in love with Bianca – really in love with her, it feels like … But at the same time, he can't really stand her history with Mikko.'

'Mikko, again.'

'The prompter, Ursula Andersson, saw him coming out of Bianca's dressing room last week, the same day her dress caught fire.'

'Which means Ursula was also there.'

'Absolutely, but I've double-checked and she really had been admitted for surgery at the Karolinska the night someone broke into Bianca's apartment. I don't know. Ursula seems like someone who has been beaten down by life, by circumstance. She's so shy now, almost reclusive, but there's something about her … I really feel she could be holding on to vital information.'

They watched Bianca douse her cigarette beneath the tap, then throw the butt into the rubbish bin and leave the kitchen.

'Is that everyone?' asked Sid.

'No, there's another actor, Kerstin. I've forgotten her surname. She's sort of gone under the radar so far. Has a couple of minor parts in the upcoming production, including the witches – the same parts she took over from Bianca last time.'

The light from the little bathroom window at the end of the house shone out over the yellow flowers on the bushes outside.

'A man,' Sid said quietly.

Julia followed his gaze and saw someone standing on the footpath nearby. He was wearing loose-fitting sports clothing, and he had his hood up.

165

She handed the iPad back to Sid, who immediately started recording and turned the camera towards the man. He was standing perfectly still by the low hedge, looking towards the house. After a moment, his right hand started moving impatiently.

'Is he doing what I think he's doing?' Julia whispered.

A faint light passed through some leaves nearby, making him look cracked, like a mosaic made from pale snail shells.

Sid tried to adjust the contrast to get a better look at him. The man's hand kept moving for a moment, then stopped.

The red circle continued to pulse at the bottom of the screen.

The man took a slight step to one side, and his hand came into view as the lead he was holding pulled taut. His white terrier was trying to sniff an electricity cabinet, and the man reluctantly followed it over.

'What did you think he was doing?' Sid asked, a note of amusement to his voice.

'Taking the dog for a walk,' she replied as neutrally as she could, taking the iPad back from him.

Using the controls, she panned back across to the house and froze. Bianca and Ramon were now in the bedroom, on the bed. The actress was completely naked, straddling his hips, moving slowly with a soft smile on her lips.

For a few seconds, Julia and Sid were both completely transfixed by the dreamlike scene, then he reached over and turned off the camera.

Darkness filled the car.

Even without the camera, they could still make out the leisurely lovemaking taking place in the bedroom.

They sat side by side in awkward silence, eyes scanning the garden, the footpaths and the bushes, inevitably drawn back to the bedroom window again.

Bianca leaned forward, and Ramon cupped her breasts in his hands.

Julia would have given anything for that to be her and Sid right now.

Twenty-Seven

IT WAS TEN PAST NINE in the morning, and Ramon was leading the other actors through a warm-up exercise in rehearsal room one.

Regina was standing off to one side on the scratched black stage floor, an amethyst taped to her forehead in an attempt to ward off a headache.

Sid had taken some time off from his job with the Norrmalm Police, and he and Julia were now sitting at the production desk, talking in hushed voices.

With the head of security's blessing, the two of them had gone through the logs from the iLOQ system earlier that morning. Since everyone had their own key, and each use was tracked, it was easy to see who – in theory – could have both set Bianca's dress alight and tampered with her lighter.

As they soon discovered, that was everyone involved in the production of *Macbeth* other than Ramon and Bianca.

The prompter, Ursula, had a watertight alibi for the night of the break-in at Bianca's apartment, however, which left just Mikko, Regina, Tommy and Kerstin.

For obvious reasons, Stina Stiernstedt, who shared a dressing room with Bianca, had had the greatest number of opportunities, but she had been in London when the stalker took the cufflinks from Bianca's bedroom.

And, of course, there was still the possibility that Nicolás – or an as-yet unknown stalker – had found a way to bypass the security systems at the theatre. Julia had asked the security team to go over all of the CCTV footage to check whether anyone unauthorised had entered the building through one of the unmanned doors or goods entrances.

In any case, the number of suspects had narrowed dramatically, and Julia really felt as though the net was starting to tighten.

The actors warmed up their voices through a number of strange tongue twisters, exaggerating certain consonants and using their full tonal range.

Ursula came into the room and walked quietly around the edge of the stage, down the set of stairs and over to the mixing desk. She put down her prompt book, took a seat and turned on the reading lamp.

Regina removed the piece of tape holding the amethyst to her forehead, walked slowly across the floor and started talking to the cast about the upcoming scenes.

'Mikko, how do you feel about nudity?' she asked.

'My own?'

'I've got a vision of you stripping off in scene seven,' she explained without a shred of embarrassment. 'And then when your wife comes in and describes how you should kill the king, you're busy washing yourself ... A sort of bookend to her washing scene towards the end.'

'Yeah, sure thing,' he replied.

'Think about it, in any case.'

'Gratuitous nude scenes are the mainstay of theatre,' Bianca said in a deeply serious tone.

Sid and Julia paid close attention to the rehearsal, watching as the cast tried to implement Regina's ideas in the first few scenes.

The director emphasised that it was still early days, that her ideas were just sketches, but she did manage to achieve a few suggestive moments – like when Mikko and Ramon came rolling onto the stage together, over to Bianca's feet.

"*Let your Highness command upon me,*" Banquo said to Macbeth. "*To the which my duties are with a most indissoluble tie forever knit.*"

After two hours, the actors gathered in a circle around Regina in the middle of the stage, chatting among themselves and playing some sort of closing game.

'I've just heard back from Statistics Finland,' Sid whispered, leaning in to Julia with his phone in his hand. 'They've confirmed that Nicolás is dead. The time and place are a match.'

'Let's hold off on sharing that for now,' she said, reaching for her cane.

'OK.'

'What was the cause of death?'

'Private citizens can't request death certificates unless they're related to the deceased.'

'But you can, as a police officer?'

'This isn't a police matter, though.'

'This isn't a police matter, though,' she parroted in a high-pitched voice.

'It's not,' he said, his face serious.

'It's not,' she repeated.

'Julia, I know you just want to help Bianca, but these rules are there to protect people's privacy,' he said patiently.

'Why change the rules at Wimbledon and let the women wear dark underwear? Wouldn't it be easier just to ban periods?'

The actors gave a round of applause and then headed over to the wig and mask department with Regina to meet the costume designer. Ursula and the stage manager stayed behind, chatting quietly over by the mixing desk.

Julia and Sid got to their feet and made their way up onto the stage.

'I'm not sure what Bianca has planned for this evening, but we probably shouldn't hang around outside Ramon's place again,' she said with a smile. 'Though on the other hand, if she's going to be at home, it would be good if we were there.'

'I can't tonight, I'm afraid.'

'I thought you'd taken some time off?'

'It's just tonight, I . . .'

He trailed off and glanced over to the stage manager, who was laughing at something Ursula had shown her on her phone.

'You're seeing Doreen?' asked Julia.

'Yes,' he replied without looking at her.

'That's great, really . . . I . . . I don't know what to say.'

'I can cancel if—'

'No, don't be silly.' She cut him off. 'No . . . I'll be fine on my own.'

'You're Julia Stark.'

She shook her head and tried to compose herself before she went on. 'You know I want you to be happy.'

'Thanks,' he whispered.

'Sorry,' she said, trying to blink back the tears.

Ursula and the stage manager came up onto the stage and continued to chat as they left the room.

'You don't need to hang around to talk to Mikko, you know,' said Julia.

Sid raised an eyebrow. 'Is that your way of saying you want me to go?' he asked.

'I don't know . . . I just feel like I might get distracted with you here.'

'OK.'

'Let's speak tomorrow.'

'Be careful this evening,' he said.

Julia watched him go, and she realised she probably should have said the same thing to him – be careful this evening – but in reference to her own heart, and the fragile closeness that had grown between them since she had managed to bring him back into her life.

At a quarter to twelve, the cast gathered around the table the set designer had wheeled into the room. He had built a scale model of the main stage, around eighty centimetres wide and almost as deep. The floor and backdrop resembled an abandoned battlefield, littered with dead bodies, scavenging crows and bare trees. The ravaged landscape stretched out towards the horizon in a kind of never-ending grey monotony. And in the middle of the stage – providing a surreal element to the production – there was an enormous dice.

'I've based it on Scotland in early spring, before the buds come out. The ground glitters with frost at night,' the set designer explained, pushing his glasses up onto the bridge of his nose. 'The war has been devastating, but the tragedy hasn't even begun.'

'Beautiful,' Bianca whispered.

'This represents rolling the dice of fate,' he continued, pressing a finger to the huge dice. 'It'll measure four metres across, and it can function as whatever we need it to be: a fortress, a ballroom, a bloody chamber, and so on.'

Bianca clapped a hand to her mouth in astonishment, and Julia noticed that she had a small lipstick stain on her sleeve.

Mikko pressed a hand to the base of Ursula's spine as he leaned in to the model. 'This is a guaranteed hit,' he said sarcastically. 'Everyone in Sweden loves theatre.'

'I doubt half the population even knows what theatre means,' the set designer replied.

'Yeah, the men,' suggested Regina.

'Amen.' Ursula laughed, moving away from Mikko.

'That's a bit unfair, if you ask me,' he said. 'I remember when I was part of a fringe theatre group, we got a request from the boss of a pretty big company ... They wanted to hire male actors to dress up as women and serve drinks at their party.'

Twenty-Eight

JULIA AND MIKKO WERE NOW alone in rehearsal room one, and they sat down with their coffees at the table that had been carried out into the middle of the stage.

With her cane resting against her thigh, Julia thanked him for finding the time to chat. She then explained that she needed to map out the movements of everyone around Bianca in order to investigate whether anyone could have seen anything that might be a key piece of the puzzle.

'It could be anything. The most minor of details, things you don't remember until you're asked a direct question about them,' she explained.

Mikko seemed to accept the premise of their chat and said that at the time Bianca's dress was set alight, he was in his own dressing room, talking to his agent on the phone and then replying to a German email interview.

'And you didn't visit anyone else's dressing room?' asked Julia.

'No, why would I?'

'Do you know about Bianca's secret smoking habit?'

'Everyone does.'

'Did you see anyone in the corridor when you were going to or from your dressing room?'

'Can't remember.'

Julia shifted her focus to the second timeframe. Bianca had smoked a cigarette at 9.50 a.m., before the rehearsal, and they had discovered that the lighter had been tampered with at 11.45. That left a window of one hour and fifty-five minutes.

Thanks to the iLOQ system, Julia knew that Tommy had been in the corridor during that period. Kerstin had too, but not Ramon.

Stina Stiernstedt, who shared Bianca's dressing room, had been taking part in an experimental production in Gothenburg at the time, giving her a double alibi.

Julia knew that Mikko had been in the corridor between 11.05 and 11.20, but she asked the question anyway.

'Just after eleven? Don't remember,' he replied.

'You all took a break after you accidentally knocked Bianca over,' she clarified.

'Right ... No, I didn't make it over to the dressing rooms then.'

'You were late getting back to rehearsals, though.'

'Yeah, I lost track of time. Got chatting to a friend in the canteen.'

'Who?'

'That's private,' he said.

'And you're sure you didn't go to your dressing room during the break?'

'Yup, I'm sure.'

Julia studied Mikko, thinking back to the moment when he shoved Bianca, the frightened look on her face as she fell and his irritation when he thought Regina and Bianca were having a go at him.

After that, he had gone straight to the corridor where both he and Bianca had a dressing room, yet here he was claiming he hadn't.

'Let's rewind a few years, to the period just before the premiere last time,' said Julia.

'I was fucking great,' he said with a grin.

'So I've heard ... but I'm more interested in something that happened at Riche.'

He tore open the wrapper of a protein bar, ate it in two bites and chewed for a moment.

'Do you know what I'm getting at?' she asked.

'Look, I'm a passionate man,' he replied. 'I sometimes get carried away.'

'Do you remember what happened?'

'I was exhausted, not enough sleep, too much to drink ... Story of all my proudest moments, you know?' he said with a weary smile. 'But then I saw Bianca's big eyes, her smile and her proud chin. I forgot there were a bunch of other people around us ... and before I knew it, I got a well-deserved smack.'

A woman with pink hair, dark roots and thick brows came into the room. She looked all around, apologised for intruding, and said that Ramon was due in costume.

'Have you seen him?' she asked.

'Not since the set designer was here,' Mikko replied.

The woman left the rehearsal room, and Mikko took a sip of his coffee before slowly lowering the cup to the table.

'Bianca can be unbelievably flirty one minute and completely different the next ... I'm a man, and it works on me every single time. But I know that's no excuse for my behaviour.'

'Are you still in love with her?'

He threw his hands out in an over-the-top shrug. 'Was I ever?'

'You helped her get a foot in the door here, straight out of drama school,' Julia reminded him.

'Yeah, I recognise talent when I see it.'

Julia blew on her coffee and took a hesitant sip.

'How do you handle being dumped, rejected, despised?' she asked.

'I don't even know what those words mean,' he replied with a grin and a jokey frown.

'I'm serious.'

Mikko leaned back in his chair, clasped his hands behind his neck and studied Julia with his pale eyes. 'I'm a romantic.'

'Which essentially means all or nothing,' she said.

He held her gaze with a soft smile that let her know he had no intention of saying any more.

'OK, Mikko ... I know enough to know that you've been stalking Bianca,' she said. 'And I'm wondering if—'

'Are you accusing me of something?' He cut her off, straightening up.

'Yes.'

'On what grounds?'

'I could call the police.'

'OK ...'

'But it would be better if you just owned up,' she continued.

'To what?' Mikko asked with a sceptical smile.

'You couldn't accept the fact that Bianca had chosen someone else, that she was faithful to her fiancé. You felt manipulated, used ... and that only got worse after she became a star, becoming unbearable when her name ended up above yours in the promo for this production.'

'That was Regina's decision,' he muttered.

'You were in Bianca's dressing room the night her dress caught fire, yet you claim you didn't go back down there after you pushed her over.'

'Yeah, because I didn't.'

'You weren't in the corridor between five past and twenty past eleven?'

'I told you, I was in the canteen.'

Julia leaned towards him. 'But I know you were in the corridor, Mikko,' she said. 'The iLOQ system logs everyone's movements around the building.'

Twenty-Nine

IKKO NODDED CALMLY, AND JULIA felt a sense of unease flood through her, a tidal wave of icy water. She broke off eye contact and looked down at the chipped black paint on the stage floor, at the black curtains and the brick wall.

The chair creaked under Mikko's weight as he rocked back on two legs. 'You weren't the one who solved the china dolls case,' he said.

'I was,' she said, looking up at him again.

'It was your cop buddy, wasn't it?'

'No, I was working alone.'

He raised a sceptical eyebrow. 'You know it's possible to lend someone your key, right?' he said. 'And if someone else has my key, the iLOQ system will think it's me moving about the building.'

'Have you lent someone your key?'

'Yeah.'

'Who?'

'Ramon.'

'Why?'

'His dressing room's on the next floor down, and he needed to do something in mine.'

'Something,' Julia repeated, gripping her cane.

'So we swapped,' he rounded off.

'Why didn't you just tell me that from the start?'

He shrugged.

'I'll have to verify this with Ramon,' Julia warned him.

'He's still got my key, and I've got his.'

'Then how did you get into your dressing room this morning?'

'I didn't. I only really use it ahead of a performance,' he said.

Julia sighed and took out her phone, then called down to reception and explained who she was – despite the fact that she had seen the receptionist earlier that morning.

'I'm sorry to bother you,' she continued.

'It's no problem at all,' said the woman.

'Would you be able to log in to iLOQ and check where Ramon Breiner is right now?'

'One moment. He's . . . in rehearsal room one, with you.' The receptionist sounded confused.

'Are you sure?'

'Isn't he there?'

'Ah yes, I see him now. Sorry again for bothering you,' Julia said, quickly ending the call.

She dropped her phone back into her bag, took a deep breath and met Mikko's calm blue eyes.

'OK, I'm sorry to have accused you of—'

'Forget it,' he said.

'I was wrong. I'm sorry.'

He looked deep into her eyes, then slowly reached out and ran his rough thumb over her lips. As though in a nightmare, Julia pushed her chair back, heart racing. 'Don't do that,' she managed to whisper.

'You're really fucking beautiful, you know,' he said, moving towards her again. 'You're—'

'Stop!' she shouted, leaping up and knocking her coffee cup over.

'OK, sorry,' he said, holding up both hands and letting out a faux laugh. 'Jesus.'

Julia stood perfectly still, breathing rapidly, overcome by the paralysing sensation of cold blood on her skin, of being trapped among broken, lifeless bodies.

'It's good you're so clear, hey?' he said.

At the bottom of the steep mountainside, there were pieces of wreckage, twisted metal and burning plastic. It felt as though there was blood running down her throat, and she had to cough, pressing a hand to her mouth as she slowly returned to the present.

'Sit down.'

'Sorry,' she whispered.

'Guess we've both made a mistake now,' Mikko said softly. 'Sit down, please.'

Julia nodded and took a seat, conscious that her thighs had started shaking almost spasmodically as her muscles relaxed. She waited a moment, then put her hands on the table in front of her and swallowed.

'What was this "thing" Ramon wanted to do in your dressing room?' she asked, confident that he would tell her the truth.

Viewed purely in terms of his actions, Mikko was a relatively straightforward person. He was driven by an insatiable need for affirmation from other men, and their response was all that really mattered. The why was completely opaque to him.

'I'd hooked him up with a pack of Abstral, and he needed somewhere to shoot up. I'm the only one who doesn't have to share a dressing room.'

'Are you telling me Ramon is an addict?'

'He's a user, for sure.'

Julia took a moment to process what he had just said, rapidly rearranging a few pieces of the puzzle before pushing ahead with her questions. 'How would you describe your relationship with Bianca these days?'

'Good . . . We work well together, have great chemistry, but we're just friends. There's nothing sexual going on. We tried that, got it over and done with early on.'

'And what about the incident at Riche? How was your friendship then? Are you telling me there was nothing sexual about your actions that night?'

'Look, I might not always have the best judgement . . .' he explained.

'Mmm . . . I think I can speak for all women when I say that no one wants their breasts exposed in a bar.'

'No.'

'And you ended up with a "well-deserved smack" from another man.'

Mikko ran a hand through his hair. The gesture wasn't one of vanity, just his way of winning himself a few seconds. 'I was drunk, so I didn't realise what was going on at first . . . Suddenly I was on the floor, and I'd knocked Bianca's bag over in the process. Makeup, keys, condoms and tampons all over the place . . . I could've taken him, though. I would've beaten the shit out of him.'

'But you didn't,' Julia said after a brief pause.

'No.'

'Because the others intervened?'

'I got back up and started talking about how I know people in the underworld, how I could put a price on his head, but if I'm really honest the whole thing was a bit of a turning point for me ... Deep down, I thought I probably deserved it, like I said.'

'Shouldn't it have been Bianca who hit you?'

Mikko leaned towards Julia, and she had to make a real effort not to recoil.

'I apologised at the crisis meeting, and then I voted to go ahead with the premiere, just like she did ... along with Regina and whoever else was there.'

'What was this turning point you mentioned?'

'We can discuss that some other time,' he said with a smirk.

'Really?'

He looked away, towards the blue sky on the other side of the window. 'I've got the addiction gene, if such a thing really exists,' he said, turning back to her. 'I've definitely done my best to wreck my career, in any case ... And my life.'

'So there's a pattern?' said Julia.

'I grew up in Salem, my old man was a labourer. Never about, drank everything he earned. Came home every now and then, to rest, eat, sleep, fuck ... But it always ended with him screaming at Mum, hitting her, taking her money and clearing off again.'

'Did he hit you too?'

Mikko shrugged and dried a few tears from his cheeks. 'He died on a park bench in Jakobsberg when I was twenty ...

Surrounded by his junkie pals. Liver failure, officially, but he had hepatitis and syphilis, too.'

Julia showered and went through to the bedroom, where she put on a fresh sanitary pad and pulled on a pair of soft velour trousers and a vest before heading into the kitchen to put a heat pack into the microwave. She always bled a little when she ovulated, and suffered from pretty bad cramps.

At 9 p.m., the takeaway she had ordered arrived. She transferred the steaming hot food onto a plate, poured herself a glass of wine and sat down at the kitchen table.

As she ate – fried egg noodles with beansprouts and spring onions, sesame oil and dark soy sauce, broccoli and sugar snap peas – she attempted to focus on the novel she was reading, *Waiting for the Barbarians* by J. M. Coetzee. But despite the incredibly suggestive scene in which the main character ended up in a trance as he washed a young woman's feet, she just couldn't focus.

Bianca was planning to stay over at Ramon's place tonight, and Julia didn't think she needed to keep supervising their meetings.

It was true that Ramon was one of only a handful of people without an alibi, but what reason could he have to stalk the woman he was already in a relationship with? The control and jealousy angle made no sense as far as he was concerned, the break-in at her dressing room completely illogical.

It could be that he was trying to scare Bianca into turning to him for comfort, thereby becoming dependent on him, but that was undermined by the fact that he clearly valued his own independence – and his relationship with his ex-wife and kids – meaning that Bianca had to turn to people like Regina for comfort instead.

Julia couldn't rule out some other, more obscure explanation – a split personality or far-reaching projection – but she wasn't a bodyguard, and she didn't think she was likely to learn anything new by spying on them again.

She could imagine all too well how their evening might pan out, but that thought turned to anxiety when it expanded to include Sid and Doreen.

Julia opened Tinder and saw a photo of a man with handsome features and heavy eyelids. Like a Caravaggio painting, his face was a sort of lustful combination of victim and perpetrator. Julia stared at the young man and felt her palms grow clammy, and she immediately closed the app.

Thirty

J ULIA STARK WAS ALL TOO aware of what day it was as she stood in the kitchen drinking her morning coffee.

The most difficult day of the year.

Despite that, she refused to let herself call Sid, conscious that his colleague Doreen might have stayed the night.

Julia imagined them enjoying a lie in together.

They might wake around ten, have a lazy breakfast in bed, make love one more time and then grab a quick lunch before she headed off to work.

Julia moved over to the kitchen window without her cane, sipped her coffee and watched a young girl patiently waiting for a puppy as it sniffed a street cabinet beside a doorway.

Her heart rate picked up as she thought about her misstep with Mikko, the fact that she had allowed herself to get carried away and accused him of being the stalker, only to be proven wrong a moment later.

Sid should have been there by her side, she thought. It would have never happened with him there.

If she was really honest, her accusation had been more to do with Mikko's behaviour around women than anything.

It was upsetting, yes, but that didn't automatically make him guilty of the crime she was investigating.

Now, Mikko was the one with an alibi, not Ramon.

Julia knew she needed to start thinking clearly.

She couldn't understand why she had pushed Sid away. He hadn't been in a hurry to leave, had been willing to stay for the interview. They would never be able to work together in the long term if she couldn't manage to let him have a life of his own.

Julia took another sip of coffee and reminded herself that she was too good at her job to make mistakes of this kind.

She knew she should head over to the theatre, but she remained where she was in the kitchen. She had just glanced outside and seen that the girl was still waiting for her puppy when she heard the letterbox rattle.

'Thank you,' she whispered.

Julia took a deep breath, put down her cup, gritted her teeth and went through to the hallway. She bent down and picked up the postcard from the doormat, then carried it into the bedroom and opened the wardrobe.

She had spent a large chunk of her life in psychologists' offices, trying to process the trauma of the terrible plane crash that killed her family, and had now reached a stage where she was able to live in parallel with the disaster. There were days where several hours sometimes passed without her giving it a single thought. But every year, on the anniversary, Julia received a postcard without a sender or signature.

Each one had a plane on the front.

This time, it was a propellor plane. A Piper PA-28.

She put it into the shoebox with all the rest and felt a wave of anxiety rise up inside her.

Ten minutes later, she was standing by the bathroom mirror, studying the ugly lightning bolt on her cheek. Julia turned her attention to her makeup, applying concealer and a sheer layer of foundation over her scar, followed by some pale pink lipstick. She then took out an eyeliner pencil from her makeup bag and met her mother's eyes in the mirror.

Julia looked down.

'I can't take any more ...'

She dropped the pencil into the sink, turned away and steadied herself with both hands against the tiled wall, trying to breathe in the way she had been taught in therapy, conjuring up the image of herself in a photograph taken from up high in the church.

At the top edge, the lower half of the cross was visible. She saw the nails that had been driven through Jesus's feet, the blood that had trickled between his wooden toes.

And down below, the girl was sitting all alone in the front pew. The girl whose arms, legs, feet and collarbones had been put back together using titanium screws.

Her neck was being supported by a hard plastic collar.

Her crutches were on the floor in the aisle.

Four white coffins had been laid out among the choir in front of her.

Her mum, dad and two sisters.

The earthy scent of hundreds of flowers bore witness to the fleeting nature of life, to death's patient wait.

Julia's parents had met at a wedding. She was a friend of the bride, he was related to the groom. When everyone gathered outside the church ahead of the ceremony, her mother had found herself drawn to the tall, handsome man standing beside a woman and two children, and had longingly thought that she would love to meet someone like him one day. During the party that followed, she had discovered that he was single after all.

Her mother was a determined young woman who had already passed the bar, and he was a carpenter who wrote poetry. She eventually convinced him to go back to his studies.

That is one of Sweden's real strengths, Julia's mother always used to say. The fact that anyone can get an education, go to university, and be paid to do so. They can change their focus, too, starting in literature and ending up as a neurologist.

Before long, her mother was made a judge at the Svea Court of Appeal.

For some reason, their mother had gone easier on her two younger sisters, Siri and Amanda. She hadn't forced them to learn an instrument, like she had Julia. They didn't have to get straight As in every subject, nor keep their rooms neat and tidy.

Perhaps that was why Julia had snapped at them that day, on the plane from Ankara.

Her sisters had been bored, nagging Julia to challenge them in a quiz. Please, please, please, they sang in their sweet little voices.

'Do you know how boring it is to compete against two idiots?' she had replied.

Julia could still remember the disappointed look on Siri's face, the way her eyes flashed and the tip of her tongue sought out the narrow gap between her teeth.

And young Amanda, gripping her embellished phone case in one hand. Julia remembered the flicker of confusion that passed over her face, like the quick shadow of a butterfly, before she gave her the finger and started sucking on the tip of her plait.

Julia had turned her attention back to *Wuthering Heights*, completely oblivious to the fact that she would never talk to any of them again.

Thirty-One

S ID CALLED JULIA THREE TIMES as she walked to the theatre, and when she failed to pick up he sent her a text message.

I know you're going to say you want to be alone today, but I'm here to offer my professional expertise and hope you'll eat dinner with me this evening.

Due to a double booking, rehearsals had moved to the theatre's main stage.

Julia took a seat in the front of the stalls and watched as Kerstin walked out onto the stage in an untucked white shirt and a pair of jeans. She paused and gazed up at the grand art nouveau room, at the balconies and the royal box, the lavish gold flourishes and the mural of Apollo surrounded by nine muses on the ceiling.

In the sloping light, the acne scars on the actress's cheeks looked like lunar craters.

The stage manager had prepared a few simple props ahead of their rehearsal: a dining table, an armchair and a footstool. They were planning to tackle the famous scene from act three in which Macbeth sees the murdered Banquo sitting in his seat, and Regina had already been through her vision with her cast, adjusting the angle of the dining table and moving the armchair and stool a little further back.

At the front right of the stage, a director's chair and a desk chair had been placed beside the prompter's table, where a lamp illuminated the folder containing Ursula's script.

Julia double-checked that her phone was switched to silent and noticed that Sid had sent her another message, asking if he should come to the theatre.

Bianca took a swig from a can of Coca-Cola, and Mikko dropped his leather jacket onto a metal stage weight on the floor.

Regina, Ursula and Kerstin were all clutching identical white coffee cups from the staff canteen.

Ramon's eyes looked jet black, like polished carbon. He was talking to Tommy, laughing softly.

Ursula put her cup down on the dining table and went over to help carry the chairs.

Kerstin blew on her coffee, took a cautious sip and then put her cup down beside Mikko's jacket.

'This time, I want us to really dig deep into the tragedy,' said Regina. 'To make the words our own. They're not lines, OK? In our world, there is no Shakespeare.'

'Keve Hjelm gives a thumbs-up from the grave,' said Tommy, spitting a wad of snus into a rubbish bin.

'Did you ever meet him?' asked Ramon.

'Tommy's worked with everyone,' said Bianca.

Without missing a beat, Tommy treated the rest of the cast to a brief imitation of the legendary actor. He moved a few steps away, took a bow and cleared his throat.

'There shall be no dead weight on this stage, do you hear me?' he boomed, glaring at Ramon. 'I want meat on these bones, these ... boners.'

'Thanks,' Regina laughed. 'Exactly like that ...'

Bianca drank a little more of her Coke, then handed the can to Ramon. He drained the last of it, rubbed his mouth, tossed the can into the bin and burped loudly.

'Subtle,' Kerstin said with a smile.

Bianca started setting the table with plates and goblets, and moved Ursula's coffee over to the desk by her folder.

'Feel free to go all in, but don't do it just for the sake of it,' said Regina. 'Try to be present. You know what I want – no playing to the gallery ... I want you to dig deep, into the heart of the chilling realism.'

Regina handed her cup to Tommy and then applied some hand cream.

'Big, meaty boners,' said Bianca, reaching for a flagon.

Kerstin walked over to the prompter's desk and checked her lines in the script. Her mouth moved soundlessly as she read through the text, the circle of light from the lamp making her index finger glow white like a bone.

'OK ... Mikko, move back. Bianca, take a seat,' said Regina, bracelets jangling as she pointed. 'Ramon, I want you standing opposite, and ... Tommy, give my coffee back ...'

Tommy took a sip and handed her the cup.

'Thank you ... Kerstin, you're Lord Rosse in this scene.'

Kerstin nodded. She flicked her plaits back behind her shoulders, picked up a cup from the desk and took a sip, then walked over to the armchair and sat down with her feet on the footstool.

Ursula took her seat, popped a throat sweet into her mouth and adjusted the angle of the lamp.

'Go,' said Regina.

Mikko waited a few seconds, and Julia saw his face transform as he inhabited the part of Macbeth.

He took a few steps towards the table, then hesitated when Ramon – playing the murdered Banquo – slowly crossed his path and sat down in his seat.

'*The table's full,*' Mikko said, sounding confused.

'*Here is a place reserved, sir,*' Tommy replied, pointing to the chair where Ramon was sitting.

'*Where?*'

'*Here, my good lord,*' Tommy said with a smile, pointing to the taken chair again. '*What is't that moves your Highness?*'

'*Which of you have done this?*' Mikko asked, voice dripping with anxiety.

Ramon raised a hand and pointed at him, and Mikko backed away.

'*Thou canst not say I did it,*' he panted. '*Never shake thy gory locks at me.*'

There was complete silence on the stage. Kerstin had missed her line.

'*Gentlemen,*' Ursula prompted her in her croaky voice.

'Kerstin?' Regina sighed.

'*Gentlemen, rise,*' Ursula continued. '*His Highness is not well.*'

'Wakey, wakey, Kerstin!' Regina shouted.

Julia got up and saw that Kerstin was still sitting in the armchair, slumped back with her long legs outstretched and her feet on the stool.

Mikko held a finger to his lips and walked over to her with a smile, but before he reached her he stopped dead and swore.

'Call an ambulance!'

'What? What's happening?' Regina asked, getting up from her chair.

Julia quickly dialled 112, and an operator picked up as she was walking up the stairs to the stage.

'I can't find a pulse, get an ambulance here now!' Mikko shouted.

'I'm on it,' Julia replied, explaining the situation to the operator.

Bianca and Ramon helped Mikko to lower Kerstin to the floor.

'She's not breathing, she's not breathing,' Bianca whimpered.

Mikko began CPR, making Kerstin's body twitch with each thrust. Ursula was standing with a hand to her mouth, and Ramon wiped some sweat from his top lip.

'I've got an ambulance on the way,' the operator told Julia. 'Continue the CPR, and try to find out if there's a defibrillator in the building.'

'Mikko, keep doing what you're doing, the ambulance is on its way,' Julia said. 'Regina? Do you know if there's a defibrillator?'

'Tommy,' Regina responded, her voice flat. 'Do you know if—'

'I'll get it,' he shouted, running off backstage.

Thirty-Two

REHEARSALS WERE CANCELLED WITH IMMEDIATE effect, and the cast gathered by the seating area outside Wille De Geer's office for a crisis meeting the next day. Julia stood beside Ursula and the stage manager, listening to the artistic director's considered speech.

Bianca was sitting between Tommy and Regina on the green sofa, eyes lowered and a hand to her mouth.

Despite their best efforts with the defibrillator, Kerstin Tamm was dead before the ambulance even arrived. No cause of death had yet been established – it would be another three weeks until the autopsy took place – but there was talk of a stroke or a heart attack, rumours about bipolar disorder and a pill addiction.

'We're in the process of setting up a support group,' Wille de Geer continued. 'And we'll do everything we can to help you through this difficult period. With that said, I'm afraid we can't postpone the premiere, we just can't . . . So you'll have to put your heads together and decide whether to cancel the entire run or go ahead as planned.'

He mumbled an apology and then headed back into his office, closing the door behind him. Ramon performed a sarcastic salute, and Mikko stared blankly ahead, sucking in his cheeks.

After a moment, Regina got to her feet.

'Again, everyone, I'm so sorry. I don't have any encouraging words for you today ... I just can't believe it,' she said. 'It ... it's just so awful ... so, so hard ... I don't know what to say. Do any of you have any thoughts?'

'No,' Bianca mumbled.

'We can talk again tomorrow, or the next day.'

'If you ask me, we might as well get it over and done with now,' said Mikko. 'Come on, out with the feelings – we're supposed to be expressive theatre types, aren't we?'

He threw his arms up in the air and managed to knock the floor lamp, making the light bounce over the wall.

'I just want to say that I think Regina has managed to convey her vision extremely well,' said Tommy. 'I really believe in this production ... It's sharp, it's risqué.'

'I agree,' said Mikko.

'Thank you,' Regina whispered, taking a seat again.

Ramon leaned back and closed his eyes.

'Are you OK?' Bianca asked him.

'Yeah, I was just thinking about Kerstin and her son,' he said, turning to Regina. 'And ... Fuck me, this is hard.'

'Art, caught in the glare of reality,' the director said.

'To quote my own part,' Mikko spoke up, taking a deep breath. '*Life's but a walking shadow, a poor player that struts and frets his hour upon the stage and then is heard no more.*'

'We know ... But that hour, that short hour,' said Bianca, trying to hold back the tears.

Tommy reached for his water bottle on an old sewing machine table by the wall, slowly unscrewed the lid and took a swig.

Julia heard Ursula's rapid breathing beside her, saw the beads of sweat glistening on Ramon's brow. She also noticed that Regina's hands were shaking as she clasped them in her lap.

Bianca shook her head almost imperceptibly.

'So shall we make a decision?' asked Regina. 'It's up to us – what do you say? Should we call it quits?'

'No, damn it,' said Mikko.

Ramon held up a hand, licked his lips and said that he wasn't sure he would be able to really dig deep into the tragedy after this.

'Or maybe that's exactly what theatre is for,' said Tommy.

'It just feels too much right now,' Ramon explained.

Regina took a deep breath and said that she would like to keep going, to dedicate the production to Kerstin.

'Yes,' Tommy whispered.

'Bianca?' the director asked.

'I don't know, I'm going to have to abstain,' she replied, glancing up at Regina with bloodshot eyes. 'Even if, deep down, I think Kerstin would have wanted us to continue.'

Julia noticed a strange flash of cruelty in Regina's eyes, like the knife in Macbeth's hand, and she followed her gaze over to Bianca. The tip of the actress's nose had turned pink.

'That's three to keep going, one to pull the plug, and one abstention,' said Regina. 'So on the basis of that, is it OK with you, Ramon, and you, Bianca, if we try to go ahead with the premiere?'

'I guess,' Ramon replied.

Bianca gave another near-imperceptible nod.

In order to keep up the momentum, Regina decided that they would press ahead with rehearsals again after lunch, with a break for their first chats with the counsellor.

Ursula would cover Kerstin's lines and continue to prompt the others where necessary while Regina tried to find a replacement.

Julia was waiting in an armchair backstage, her cane clamped between her thighs. The emergency exit sign cast a pale green glow over the rough wall, and she heard the pipes in the ceiling clanking softly.

The door to the toilet nearby was ajar, and Julia watched in the mirror as Ursula poured some sort of clear liquid from a thermos into a paper cup.

A moment later, Bianca came down the corridor with an orange in her hand.

Ursula gargled the liquid and spat into the sink, then rinsed out her mouth with water and spat again.

'This is so tough,' Bianca said as she paused in front of Julia.

Just after one, the cast gathered around the dining table on the main stage.

One of the techs managed to knock over a pile of light filters as he moved a stepladder.

As before, Julia took a seat in the front row and watched as Mikko dragged the armchair and footstool off the stage and replaced them with an ordinary chair.

Everyone seemed subdued, introspective, but Regina kept praising them and encouraging them to take their time, to allow their grief to shine through in their performances.

Bianca's face was ashen when she got up from the table. *'Pray you, keep seat,'* she begged. *'The fit is momentary; upon a thought he will again be well . . .'*

She stopped mid-line, turned away from the others and broke down in tears. Regina went over and wrapped her arms around her. Bianca whispered that she was sorry, dried her cheeks and attempted a smile.

'Do you need a moment?' the director asked softly.

'No, no . . . it's OK, let's keep going.'

The rehearsals continued in much the same way, weighed down by a real sense of fragility, until Regina raised her voice and said that the counsellor was waiting on the sofas outside rehearsal room two.

'Bianca, do you want to go first?' she asked.

'Sure,' Bianca replied, grabbing her cardigan from the floor and disappearing backstage.

'OK everyone, let's try the last scene from act three . . . And then we'll check how the deletions from the start of the next act feel before we call it a day.'

Once rehearsals were over, Julia sat down at a table in the canteen. She ate a sandwich, scribbled down her impressions from the day and – though she was no longer sure why – ignored Sid's continued attempts to reach her.

She saw Tommy emerge from the kitchen with his arms full of plastic-wrapped sandwiches, which he put into a blue Ikea bag. As he was turning to leave, he caught Julia's eye and came over to her table.

'I take all the sandwiches that haven't sold to Sankta Clara Church, to the soup kitchen there,' he said as he lowered the bag to the floor.

'Very nice,' Julia replied with a smile.

'You learn from life.'

'I've heard that your daughter is currently homeless ... Does she go there to eat?'

'No,' he said with a sigh, taking a seat opposite Julia. 'She actually spends most of her time under the bridges in Söder at the moment, but it varies.'

'Are you worried about her?'

'Things are a bit better these days ... Whenever I have a morning off, I tend to swing by the Salvation Army. They've got a social centre over in Hornstull, and Aurora goes there to eat breakfast sometimes, to use the shower ... I always try to give her a bit of money when I see her, but she never takes more than a few notes, less than I'm offering. We chat a bit, or she listens to me talk. Obviously if it were down to me, I would've chosen a different life for her, but she's my daughter and I love her just how she is.'

He rapped his knuckles on the table, got to his feet, swung the bag up onto his shoulder and walked away.

Julia was supposed to be meeting Ramon, but he sent a message to say that he had been held up and asked if they could push it back to tomorrow instead. She got up to head home, threw her rubbish into the bin and put her mug in the tray by the sink.

As she was making her way over to the door, her phone buzzed. It was Bianca, asking Julia to come to her dressing room if she was still at the theatre.

Thirty-Three

BIANCA'S MIRROR WAS STREAKED WITH pink smears, as though it had been wiped clean in a hurry. Beneath it, her dressing table was a mess, cluttered with small pots, eyeshadow palettes, a broken powder compact in a dusty ziplock bag, a tube of moisturiser covered in grey fingerprints and a small towel stained with mascara.

On the coffee table, there was a large bouquet of red roses wrapped in cellophane, two stacks of letters held together with rubber bands, and a small heart-shaped box of chocolates.

'What happened?' asked Julia.

'Hmm? Oh, no . . . Ramon and I just had a bit of an argument.'

'What about?'

'Nothing much, it was stupid,' said Bianca.

'So what did you want to talk about?'

'I just realised that I've lost my key,' Bianca replied, looking up at her with an expression of despair.

'Which key?'

'The new one, for the apartment.'

'OK. Do you know when you lost it?'

'It must've been just now, at Café Albert . . . I was there with Ramon, and the place was packed. I went back and checked around the table, asked the staff. They said they would let me know if, you know . . .' She shrugged dejectedly.

'We'll sort it out. There's a spare, after all.'

'Sorry, I feel like I'm being so difficult . . . I was just so upset, and I rushed out of there like some stroppy teenager.'

'Do you want to talk about the argument?' asked Julia, leaning against her cane.

'It's private.'

'What I'm really getting at is whether Ramon is the jealous type,' she said.

'I don't want to talk about it,' Bianca replied, turning away.

'Because he knows about you and Mikko . . .'

'Please.'

'OK,' said Julia, waiting patiently.

There was an uncomfortable silence, then Bianca sighed. 'It was about something else.'

Julia waited again, but the actress didn't elaborate. 'Did you and Ramon have an affair in the past?'

'No.' Bianca smiled.

'Has he shown any interest in you previously?'

'Like when?'

'During rehearsals last time.'

Bianca frowned. 'What are you getting at?'

'Regina mentioned him smashing a table using a fire extinguisher.'

'I don't remember that . . . I might not have been there when that happened.'

'Is he violent?'

'Ramon? No, but I'd say he's pretty broken, as a person,' said Bianca, looking concerned but composed.

'In what sense?'

'No, forget I said anything. It's nothing.'

'Drugs?'

Bianca laughed and folded her arms. 'I have to give it to you, you really don't give up, do you?'

'It's my job to get to the truth,' Julia explained.

'The truth?'

'Yes.'

'I've been wondering whether what you said was true, about realising there was something going on between me and Ramon straight away.'

'Yes. After the stalker broke into your apartment and took the cufflinks, Ramon was the first person you rang – your first choice in the middle of the night,' Julia replied. 'You called him a colleague and said you could stay over at his place, but only when the kids weren't there – which wouldn't have mattered if he was really just a colleague.'

'Maybe . . .'

'But Ramon didn't want to risk his kids feeling uncomfortable, didn't want their mum finding out about your relationship through them.'

'You don't think he's told her?'

'What do you think?'

'Fuck,' Bianca mumbled, shaking a cigarette out of a crumpled packet.

She grabbed a cheap plastic lighter and had just moved over to the window when her phone pinged.

She picked it up from the table, read the message and turned to Julia.

'OK, Regina says she can stay over at my place tonight.'

'Great.'

Bianca climbed up onto the sofa, leaned towards the window, lit her cigarette and took a deep drag.

'But she can only come later, around eleven thirty or so. She's going to some premiere in Uppsala first,' she said, blowing the smoke out through the narrow chink.

'What are you thinking?'

'I'm sorry to ask, but do you think you and Sid could come and give the place a once-over, just to make sure everything's OK? I've checked the cameras, but this whole thing with the key is making me a bit nervous.'

'You think someone might have stolen it?'

'No, but ... I don't think so, but it's not exactly good, is it? And I know what I'm like. I won't be able to stop thinking about it.'

'When were you planning to go home?'

'In an hour or so.'

'I'll go over there now and wait for you.'

'Thank you,' Bianca whispered. Her hand was shaking as she lifted the cigarette to her lips.

Thirty-Four

J ULIA TURNED THE KEY IN the lock and heard the new
mechanism slide open with a soft metallic clang. The sound
reminded her of a sword fight in a film, she thought as she
let herself into the dark hallway.

She turned on the light, opened the coat cupboard and
pushed the hangers to one side using her cane, then moved on
to the bathroom. It was messy, with makeup, tubes, compacts
and a creamy yellow bottle of Gucci perfume in the sink. Julia
opened the shower curtain and saw a clump of hair clinging
to the edge of the tub, then went through to the living room.
After checking behind the curtains, she continued into the
kitchen. The dirty plates and glasses stacked in the sink rattled
with each step she took.

She returned to the living room and crossed the wooden
floor to the bedroom, steadying herself against the bed before
bending down to peer underneath.

Julia straightened up and opened the walk-in closet, pushing
the garment bag, dresses and coats to one side. The monitor
Sid had mounted on the wall lit up when she touched it, filling
the space with pale grey light. The screen was divided into four,
showing real-time feeds from each of the rooms. One covered

the front door and hallway, another the living room. The kitchen and balcony door were visible in the third, the bedroom in the fourth.

Julia went back through to the living room and heard the old floorboards creaking softly as she crossed the threshold. She walked straight over to the seating area, moved a couple of books and a script from the sofa and sat down.

On the cluttered coffee table, among the books and teacups, empty wine glasses, candle and bowl of salty liquorice, there was a red bra.

Julia took out her phone and wrote a message to Bianca letting her know that it was safe to come home. She then leaned back on the sofa, taking in the stacks of scripts and books on the floor, the glossy black piano and the sheet music and yet more books on the lid.

On the small side table where she had noticed a number of tarot cards last time, there was now a bouquet of flowers.

Which cards had they been? The High Priestess and the Wheel of Fortune.

Julia's eyes drifted across the framed theatre posters on the wall to the overloaded bookcase, coming to a halt when she reached the safe behind the piles of paperbacks.

She got up and walked over to it, moving two stacks of books out of the way before steadying herself against the shelf as she tried the handle.

It was locked.

She tried a few basic codes, then put the books back where she had found them and returned to the sofa.

She would have to convince Bianca to let her read the letter from Nicolás, she thought.

Right then, her phone pinged with a message.

It was from Bianca, letting her know she was running a bit late.

Julia went online to search for information about Kerstin Tamm on various forums while she waited.

It was gone ten by the time she got up and went into the kitchen to rummage through the cupboards and fridge. She found a bag of crisps and poured herself a bowl of yoghurt.

Once she had finished eating, she rinsed off the bowl, went into Bianca's bedroom and lay down on the bed. She took a few photos of the windows she could see on the far side of the street, thinking to herself that anyone standing over there would also be able to watch Bianca as she slept.

The pillow smelled like Bianca's perfume, with notes of vanilla and caramel, but she could also detect something else there. Something alluring and herbal, almost like marijuana.

Julia closed her eyes for a moment, thinking about Bianca at Ramon's place, how happy she had looked as she straddled him, how present, not having to put on any sort of act.

Bianca had had sex while she and Sid sat quietly in the car, side by side yet separated by a choppy ocean.

Doreen was probably straddling him right now, she thought. Feeling him deep inside her, his heart racing as she leans forward with her hands on his chest.

Julia opened her eyes and forced back the image, told herself there was something wrong with her, that she had to let him live his life.

She still had only a vague idea of how online dating worked, and with a real sense of unease she picked up her phone, opened an app and started scrolling through the seemingly endless stream of faces.

None of them were Sidney Mendelson.

Still, they were all touching somehow, in their own way.

A smiling man with brown eyes and an expensive-looking jacket, a pretty boy with curly blond hair. A serious man with a large nose and black stubble, a man with thin lips and tense eyes, a tattooed man with a pale face and long hair, a balding man with glasses and a full bookcase in the background. A tanned man who looked like he had been doing push-ups just before the photo was taken, a man with round cheeks and a fluffy little dog in his arms.

Each one of them quickly disappeared to the left, but Julia paused on a face that made her smile, a slightly melancholy sensation in her chest.

Charley
39
'Complete beginner'
Architect
Lives in Stockholm
Less than four kilometres away

The image was of a clean-shaven man with warm eyes and thick, messy hair. He had probably been extremely cute as a child, but the years had taken their toll on him, grief leaving its mark on his face.

Complete beginner at this dating malarkey, but my friends and darling ex are making me give it a go . . .

Julia hadn't even finished reading before she swiped right, and she felt a rush of red-hot embarrassment when she immediately got a message announcing 'It's a match!'

It took a real effort to stop herself from closing the app and deleting it from her phone, and she took a moment to study Charley's face before she started writing a message to him: *Sorry, but I don't think this is going to work.*

Julia erased the message, closed her eyes and started thinking about a yellow plastic bucket full of small red apples. Sid had picked them from the tree in his mum's allotment garden, and had been boyishly excited about the prospect of using them to bake an apple pie.

Julia woke with a start at the sound of clashing swords, the noise the new lock mechanism made when it turned.

Her heart was racing.

She had fallen asleep on Bianca's bed.

The bedroom was almost pitch black.

Bianca really was running late, she thought, though a moment later she remembered that the actress didn't have a key.

Julia pricked up her ears.

The apartment was quiet. Maybe she hadn't heard anything.

She reached for her phone. It was half-one in the morning, and Bianca had sent a message just before eleven to say that she was going to stay over at Ramon's place after all.

Julia sat up. She had just decided to call for a taxi and head home when she heard the hinges on the glass door between the hall and the lounge creak.

There was someone else in the apartment.

Holding her breath, she got to her feet, grabbed her cane and heard the plates on the kitchen counter rattle softly.

She made her way over to the walk-in closet as quietly as she could, pulling the door shut behind her. On the pale video monitor, she could see a black-clad figure in a balaclava. One of the cameras caught him as he left the kitchen, and a moment later he reappeared in the living room.

Julia dialled 112, then turned the brightness and sound right down before she made the call and put her phone on the shelf to one side of the monitor.

The floorboards in the bedroom creaked.

Julia gripped her cane with both hands.

She couldn't hear the stalker, but she watched him on the monitor as he bent down to check beneath the bed before turning towards the camera.

She heard a series of quick footsteps, and the door to the closet flew open. Julia tried to use her cane to defend herself, but she was dragged out and lost her balance, cracking her head against the dresser as she fell.

Thirty-Five

I T WAS 10 A.M. WHEN Julia sat down at the computer in her office to start writing up everything she could remember from the night before.

She hadn't got home from the hospital until five, and then she had jumped in the shower, taken half a sleeping pill and slept until nine.

She wasn't sure whether she had passed out for a moment or two in the closet, but by the time she managed to get back onto her feet the stalker was already on his way out of the apartment, and a second later she heard the front door slam.

Julia had grabbed her cane and hurried to lock the door, in tears because she had got such a fright. Reaching up to touch the back of her head, she had noticed there was blood on her fingers.

Right then, she remembered her phone and made her way back into the closet. The operator was still on the line, and she explained what had happened.

A car was already on its way, the operator told her.

It arrived ten minutes later.

A confused Julia had answered the officers' questions as best she could, and then they had driven her to A&E.

She had woken to the sound of the lock mechanism clicking.

The most likely explanation was that someone had stolen Bianca's key from her bag while she and Ramon were arguing in Café Albert.

Julia leaned back in her chair with a sigh.

She had her breakfast on a tray beside the computer: a large glass of freshly-squeezed orange juice and a toasted sandwich filled with smoked ham, Dijon mustard, lettuce, beansprouts, cheese and chilli sauce.

It was something her father always used to make for her and her sisters, calling it 'Daddy's Sandwich Rocket,' without further explanation.

She picked up the sandwich, folded back the greaseproof paper and took a bite, losing herself for a moment in the sense of calm the combination of flavours brought her.

Once she had finished her breakfast, she began jotting down everything she could remember about the stalker based on what she had seen on the monitor in the closet and how she had felt when he knocked her over.

The masked intruder had moved quickly and with ease, as though he knew his way around, but Julia wasn't entirely sure what the purpose of the break-in had been. It hadn't seemed as though he was looking for anything but Bianca.

She hadn't seen a weapon, and Julia had just written that that could indicate confidence in his physical superiority when her phone started ringing. She felt butterflies in her stomach as Sid's face flashed up on the screen.

'Good morning ... or whatever it is,' she said.

'What the hell do you think you're playing at?'

'Sorry?'

'First, you break off all contact and then—'

'I thought you were busy,' she replied.

'No you didn't. I texted you, I called, I—'

'I don't need your pity.' She cut him off.

'Julia, I'm trying to trust you, but you're making it impossible. You're putting yourself in danger – real danger – and all because I went on a date. It's honestly insane.'

'Don't be mad at me,' she begged him.

'What the hell did you expect? He could have killed you, do you understand that?'

'Don't shout,' she said, breaking down in tears.

'I'm a good detective, a good investigator. I thought you needed my help, but this . . . It's just so fucking unprofessional, and I don't think I can keep working with you if—'

Julia hung up, went back through to her apartment and slumped down onto the bed. She buried her face in the pillow and cried.

The scar on Julia's cheek was still flushed when she got to the half-empty staff canteen at the theatre, her eyes puffy and sensitive. Bianca was waiting for her at a table in the back left-hand corner, her handbag on the pale brown leather sofa beside her.

The brass lamp on the wall to one side of her cast a warm glow across her concerned face, her hands on the table and the bowl of salad in front of her.

Julia made her way over and took a seat opposite the actress. She pushed the spare key across to Bianca and said that they would need to change the locks again.

'Sorry for making you go over there and wait for me,' Bianca replied, dropping the keys into her bag. 'I ended up going to this crazy performance involving live sheep, a masturbating tramp and naked actors on a conveyor belt, and then I went home with Ramon and forgot all about you ...'

'It's OK,' Julia replied. 'But I need you to check the camera feeds for me.'

Bianca frowned and took out her phone. 'What's going on?'

'I fell asleep at your place, and when I woke up the stalker was there.'

Bianca gasped and stared at her with wide eyes. 'Jesus ... What happened?'

'I hid in the closet and ... well, you'll see.'

Julia pushed the little tray holding the salt and pepper shakers to one side and leaned forward.

Bianca's hands were shaking as she opened the app and stared down at the live feed of her apartment.

'Try the recording from the hallway first. Around one thirty this morning.'

From its position close to the ceiling, the camera had caught the front door opening and someone wearing a balaclava entering the apartment. The figure passed the mirror on the wall and walked slowly out of view.

Bianca whimpered.

The motion-activated feed then jumped forward four minutes, to the moment the intruder rushed back out of the apartment.

'Next room,' said Julia.

Bianca quickly switched to the recording from the living room, and the two women watched as the stalker first walked slowly past the window, then ran back in the other direction.

In the feed from the kitchen, they got only a brief glimpse of him: a dark shadow passing through and then turning around. The last recording was considerably longer.

The camera in the bedroom was angled towards the window, but thanks to its high placement and wide-angle lens, most of the room was visible.

'God . . .' Bianca whispered.

They watched as Julia woke on the bed, sat up, looked down at her phone and then slumped to the floor, grabbed her cane and hurried into the closet.

The figure in black came into the room, walked over to the window and checked behind the curtain. He then bent down, looked beneath the bed and walked towards the closet, pausing for a moment before opening the door and stumbling back as Julia lashed out with her cane.

The intruder's movements were quick and supple, catching Julia's arm, pulling her forward and knocking her down.

The camera caught Julia doing a half-flip, hitting the floor and banging the back of her head on the dresser.

'Jesus, are you OK?' Bianca asked, looking up at Julia.

'I'm fine . . . Just a few bruises,' she mumbled.

On the feed, the stalker then rushed out of the room. Julia got to her feet and reached for her cane, stood still for a few seconds, then wandered out of shot as though in a daze.

'You need to talk to the police, you need—'

'I already have.' Julia cut her off. 'They came to the apartment. But there wasn't much they could do.'

Bianca looked scared, and a number of red blotches had flared up on her cheeks.

'But what did they say? What should I—'

'I'll get to that, but right now I need you to scroll back through the footage, to just after the stalker looks under the bed . . . I think that's the best shot we've got of him.'

'OK.'

She did as Julia had said, pausing the video and then replaying it frame by frame. The intruder got to his feet and glanced up at the closet, turning so that he was almost staring straight at the camera.

The opening in his balaclava looked like a pale, horizontal rectangle.

'Could you enlarge that?'

Bianca zoomed in on the man's face until it started to lose its sharpness. Despite that, and despite the balaclava, it was possible to see the bridge of his nose, his eyes, brows and general face shape beneath the black fabric.

'That's Nicolás,' she whispered. 'Those are Nicolás's eyes. It's him, I told you . . .'

'Take a screenshot.'

'It's him, it's Nicolás,' she repeated.

'Take a screenshot and send it to me. Copy the videos and send them to me, too.'

'Why is he doing this?'

Thirty-Six

BEFORE BIANCA HURRIED OFF TO her next session with the counsellor, Julia managed to convince the actress to at least consider letting her read the letter in her safe.

She then stayed behind at the table in the canteen, rewatching the footage from the security cameras on her phone.

Around fifteen minutes earlier, Mikko had come in with a journalist and a photographer, and they were sitting at one of the tables by the windows looking out onto Berzelii Park.

Julia found herself thinking about the theatre building as a bleak representation of the social hierarchy.

The grand facade, the crystal chandeliers, velvet seats and gold décor were something that had once been reserved for the aristocracy.

Below that came the refurbished areas that only a select handful of people – journalists and various cultural figures, for example – ever got to see: the staff entrance, the stairwell, the artistic director's office and this canteen.

The rest of the interior was drab and well past its best – and beneath all that, of course, there was yet another layer, containing the cleaning carts, refuse room and sewers.

Julia had just stood up to get herself another cup of coffee when she noticed Sid in the doorway. She leaned heavily against her cane and lowered her eyes as he started walking towards her, focusing on the patch of sunlight quivering on the tiles by her feet. She was afraid she might start crying if she looked up and saw the disappointment on his face.

'Sorry,' she mumbled when he reached her. 'I promise ...'

She trailed off as he wrapped his arms around her, and she stood quietly in his embrace. Sid held her for a long time and then kissed her on the top of her head.

'I was scared, that's all,' he said softly. 'You have to stop being so reckless, doing such stupid things. You get that, don't you?'

Looking back later, she would almost think it was worth being knocked down by a stalker just to relive that moment, that embrace, those precious few seconds before they pulled apart and sat down at her table.

As the canteen slowly filled up, they watched the videos from Bianca's security cameras together. Sid gently rubbed Julia's back when they got to the part where she was thrown to the floor.

Julia rewound the footage from the bedroom and paused at the moment when the stalker checked beneath the bed. She then slowly moved forward, frame by frame, until he looked straight at the camera.

'Bianca is convinced it's Nicolás,' she said.

'When are you going to tell her about the death certificate?'

'Soon.'

'I can reach out to Johan at the National Crime Unit to see if he can do anything to improve the quality, or use this to produce a composite image,' said Sid.

'Yes, please.'

'Let's watch it all again.'

Julia pressed play on the clip from the hall, when the stalker first snuck into the apartment. She had just woken to the sound of the lock, and hurried into the closet to hide.

The clinking of cutlery and china in the canteen faded, and Julia felt a tingle between her legs as she became weightless. The fair hair on her forearms stood on end.

She looked down at Sid's tanned hand, which cupped hers to steady the phone and adjust the angle.

His short nails and rounded fingertips, no smooth gold ring on his ring finger.

The stalker hurried back through the hall.

Julia saw his eyes and the pale rectangle of skin exposed by his balaclava flicker by in the mirror.

In the next clip, he slowly made his way into the kitchen, returned to the living room and turned towards the bedroom.

Sid seemed to stop breathing, and the room was completely silent.

Julia felt as though she was underwater as she reached out with her other hand and tapped the screen, barely conscious of what she was doing.

She started the first clip again, staring at the stalker as he snuck into the hallway and pausing the footage as he returned following his confrontation with her.

The camera, mounted high on the wall, had caught him from behind.

In the mirror, Julia could see his black glove and what looked like a bruise on the small chink of skin visible at his wrist. She took in the bobbled cuff of his windbreaker and the shiny silver logo on the shoulder, the pale skin at the base of his throat and the moisture on his balaclava where it covered his mouth. The shape of his nose beneath the fabric, his wide eyes and the curve of his skull.

She had just zoomed in on the image when time regained its normal speed and she dropped back down onto the chair.

'God . . .' she whispered.

The noise of the canteen hit her like a tidal wave, the whirr of the coffee machine almost deafening. Over the speaker system, a voice announced that rehearsals for *Magnus Rex* would be starting in ten minutes.

Julia looked down at the phone in her hand again, at the gleam from the wall lamp on the screen and the stalker's reflection in the hallway mirror.

She had zoomed in on his right hand.

The bruise on his wrist was, in fact, a tattoo. One that looked like three angular rooftops piled one on top of another, like a stack of pagodas.

'He's a soldier. A sergeant,' said Sid.

'*She* is,' Julia whispered. 'She's a soldier.'

'What?'

'It's Nicolás's sister. She's a peacekeeper with the United Nations.'

Thirty-Seven

THE DARK FIGURE CAUGHT ON camera in Bianca's apartment wasn't Nicolás; it was someone with such similar eyes that they could be mistaken for his.

Julia had already known that his sister was part of the UN peacekeeping force in South Sudan, and once Sid recognised the tattoo as being military in nature, the intruder's identity suddenly seemed so obvious.

She ran a quick background search on Lovisa Castelo in order to provide Sid with as much information as possible ahead of their first exchange following her arrest and in the crucial hours that followed.

Lovisa had been reading international law at Cambridge University when she broke off her studies after some sort of scandal – a scandal that had been hushed up thanks to a donation from the family, or so Julia read between the lines. She had then moved to Sweden, where she spent a while hanging out with Nicolás. Her parents had bankrolled her through this period, but after a falling-out of some kind she had cut all ties and enlisted as a soldier.

After one year stationed in Mali and three in South Sudan, she was clearly back in Sweden.

Sid started planning for the police operation, and Julia reminded him that he had to insist on conducting the first interview with Lovisa because he knew more about her than anyone else on the force.

'You'll only get one shot,' Julia emphasised. 'Lovisa feels invincible right now, but everything will start to unravel once she's arrested – though she still won't be able to see the consequences of her actions, which means . . . which means she'll talk if you ask the right questions before the prosecutor and solicitor get involved.'

She gave Sid clear instructions for the initial interview, things he should look out for and memorise, things he should ask and in which order – depending on Lovisa's answers.

'Assuming it really is her, assuming she has a tattoo on her wrist, I don't think it'll be hard to get a confession out of her,' Julia went on. 'You should tell her that she was caught on camera in Bianca's apartment pretty much straight away. Tell her that's how you were able to identify her.'

'I'll try.'

'But what you really need to focus on before the prosecutor or her legal representative get in the way is her means and motive, and whether she's been working with anyone else.'

'OK.'

'You know how I like to ask questions, that I don't give in, even if it gets uncomfortable. And that I can usually manage to do it without being confrontational.'

'I know, but—'

'Just pretend you're Julia Stark.'

'Ha. OK, I'll try.'

'Sid, I know you can do this.'

'Not like you, but . . .'

'Just don't forget to ask her why. Ask what right she had to break into Bianca's apartment.'

'OK.'

'I'm guessing she'll say something . . . I don't know, something kind of rhetorical about Bianca going about her life like nothing happened, even though Nicolás is dead . . . and then – and remember this – you'll need to ask her to go on, to act like you're genuinely interested, as though you're giving her the benefit of the doubt.'

Lovisa Castelo lived in a quiet residential area in Täby, around fifteen kilometres north of central Stockholm.

It was six thirty in the evening when a black van pulled up outside one of the mint green houses.

Lovisa's car was plugged in to charge on the driveway.

An elderly woman was washing her own car nearby, the thick foam running into one of the storm drains.

Children played basketball and rode skateboards along the tranquil street. The air smelled like summer, heavy with the scent of flowers, sun-warmed tarmac and barbecues.

A bearded man walked by with a pushchair, talking on the phone.

Sid and five other officers, all dressed in plain clothes with protective vests underneath, approached the house from three directions.

Sid had an empty box from a delivery firm under one arm.

Once his colleagues were in position, he and a female officer walked up to the door and rang the bell.

On the other side of the low rose bushes, an old man with bluish lips and liver spots on his face was using a strimmer to cut the long grass around the edge of a paved area.

The loud whirring stopped abruptly, and a strange silence descended over the street.

Sid and his colleague waited a moment, then rang the bell again. The shrill sound reached them through the door, and they saw movement through the gap at the edge of the salmon pink curtain.

They heard shuffling footsteps, then the lock clicked and the door opened. Lovisa was a tall, muscular woman with cropped hair. She wasn't wearing any makeup or jewellery, and was dressed in burgundy sweatpants, a T-shirt dotted with moth holes and a pair of leopard-print slippers.

A waft of fried sausages drifted out from behind her.

She looked just like her brother, but her face bore signs of anxiety and sleeplessness.

The tattoo on her wrist was fully visible.

Sid and his colleague held up their badges and asked her to turn around and put her hands behind her back.

She did as she was told without a word.

Sid then cuffed Lovisa, his colleague frisked her, and they led her over to the black van.

Thanks to the bright morning sun, Sid needed a moment for his eyes to adjust when he got to Julia's office. He then made himself a coffee, sat down opposite her and started telling her, in as much detail as he could, about Lovisa Castelo's oddly calm arrest.

As he spoke, he pushed back the sleeves of his khaki shirt and leaned in to her.

Julia thought she could detect a hint of uncertainty in his eyes, and that made her go weak at the knees.

She was wearing a cream pleated skirt and a pale crochet top, and had kicked off her wedge-heel sandals.

'OK, so you drove her over to the station for booking,' she said. 'What did you talk about during the drive?'

'Not a lot, mostly just what she could expect over the next few days.'

'Did she say much?'

'No, she was pretty quiet, just mumbled that she had no idea what was going on.'

Sid described the process of Lovisa being frisked and booked before he and his female colleague could begin the first interview.

'How did you start?' asked Julia.

'Rather than asking if she knew why we'd arrested her, I got straight to the point and explained that she'd been caught on camera in Bianca Salo's apartment.'

'Good.'

'And she seemed to accept that as a fact.'

Julia flashed him a smile.

'Try to recap the conversation exactly how it went, word for word. I want to know about every pause for breath or hesitation,' she said, leaning towards him.

'Don't think less of me,' said Sid. He seemed embarrassed, and he took out his phone. 'But I know how much you would have liked to be there, so I accidentally set my phone

231

to record ... I know that's not allowed, so I'm wondering if you might be able to help me delete the file.'

'Of course.'

'I'll go out for a walk while you're doing that.'

Thirty-Eight

J ULIA KNEW ALL TOO WELL how hard Sid found it to break the rules, and she knew what it did to his self-image.

She reached for his phone and pressed play on the recording the minute he left her office.

Against a backdrop of scraping chair legs, she heard a muffled voice telling everyone to take a seat, to help themselves to water.

A woman then explained that the interview was being filmed and recorded before taking Lovisa through her various rights and rounding off by introducing everyone in the room.

'You were caught on camera in Bianca Salo's apartment,' Sid said in a neutral voice.

'I just went to pick up a few things that don't belong to her,' Lovisa replied.

'If that's true, shouldn't one visit have been enough?'

'I couldn't find Nicolás's watch.'

'So you stole her keys,' Sid continued.

'She'd had the locks changed.'

'You stole her keys while she was at Café Albert in order to access her apartment and take things that aren't hers?'

'More or less.'

'Why?' asked Sid.

'Why? Why is my big brother dead?'

'I don't know. Tell me what you think,' Sid pressed her, doing his best to sound friendly, interested.

The microphone crackled.

'I'll say this,' Lovisa replied. 'Less than four years ago, I was just north of Kodok, not far from the Sudan border. I borrowed a satellite phone from my commander and called Nicolás . . . He was upset, to put it mildly, and even though he was trying to sound mature, saying that he knew it wasn't possible to make someone love him, I could hear that he was crying when he said that he didn't think Bianca would ever be able to fully let go of Mikko.'

'Are you suggesting they were having an affair?' Sid asked.

Lovisa let out a deep sigh. 'That was something we'd argued about before . . . Look, I'll be blunt: I thought Bianca was a whore. She slept with Mikko to get a job at Dramaten. She actually told my brother that. But Nicolás stood up for her, said she'd been manipulated, that she was the victim. So I said fine, let's wait and see . . . Maybe that was wrong of me, but I didn't want to see him get his heart broken.'

'Of course,' Sid said, in an attempt to keep her talking.

'Anyway, as I was sitting there with the satellite phone at one in the morning, hearing the autocannons and rockets going off . . . he told me that Bianca and Mikko were going to be in a production together for the first time, *Macbeth*. She'd started coming home late every night, being weird about letting him see her phone, you know . . . And it was making Nicolás feel like shit. He'd tried asking her if there was something going on with Mikko, but she denied everything.'

Lovisa's voice broke and she cleared her throat. It sounded like someone passed her a cup of water, and she took a few sips before she went on. 'He wasn't sleeping. And then, in Helsinki . . . I think it all just got too much for him that night, after she went back to Stockholm, to Mikko, and . . . and he took a bit too much of his powder.'

'Have you seen his death certificate?' asked Sid.

'What? No.'

'What did you mean by powder?'

'A couple of years before he died, he mentioned that he couldn't sleep because Bianca was away on tour, so I told him what I usually take when I'm in the field . . . You know, when I really need to sleep, despite all the gunfire and shouting.'

'What do you take?'

'There are far more potent combinations, but I usually take twenty-five milligrams of promethazine, twenty of zopiclone and eight milligrams of melatonin,' she said with a hint of amusement in her voice. 'But Nicolás couldn't swallow pills, so he had to crush them first, then mix the powder into yoghurt or something.'

'And this is something he took on a regular basis?'

'Yeah, from time to time.'

'What do you think happened in Helsinki?'

'It doesn't matter what I think. Maybe something happened to upset him, and he took way too much powder. Or maybe he got blind drunk . . . Either way, there's one thing I know for sure, and that's that he would still be alive if Bianca hadn't been a whore. She completely broke him.'

'You think his death was her fault,' Sid suggested.

'One hundred per cent.'

'Was that why you wrote to her using Nicolás's Instagram account?'

There was a brief pause, then Julia heard a chair moving, someone clearing their throat.

'Good, Sid,' she whispered.

In the silence, the sound of the ventilation system was audible.

'Did you want to scare her?' asked Sid.

'All I'll say is that something inside me shifted when I saw that Dramaten was putting on *Macbeth* again, with Bianca and Mikko in the lead roles.'

'Could you elaborate?'

'Ugh, she's such a fucking whore,' Lovisa muttered.

'What did you think?' asked Sid.

'What did I think? My first thought was that she couldn't just forget about Nicolás like that . . . so I put on his red leather jacket, the one that used to belong to Schumacher. I did my hair like his, painted a dark shadow on my top lip and then went to Dramaten, sat close to the front.'

'Did she see you?'

Lovisa let out a hoarse laugh. 'See me? It was like her eyes were drawn to mine, swoosh. Straight through the fourth wall, you know? All the colour drained from her face, and she looked like she'd seen a ghost . . . That's when I knew it was true, that she'd cheated on Nicolás and was betraying him all over again. Fuck me, she looked so guilty. She started stuttering, then ran off stage. And I felt . . . I don't know, I felt like I had power over her.'

'How did you get into the theatre?'

'How do you think? I bought a ticket.'

'No, I mean ... how did you get backstage, into Bianca's dressing room? Did you have someone helping—'

'I've never been in her dressing room. What the hell are you talking about?'

Thirty-Nine

J UST A FEW SECONDS LATER, the interview was suspended when the prosecutor came into the room and took charge of the preliminary investigation. Julia heard the sound of chair legs scraping again as Sid and his colleague got up, and then the recording ended.

She deleted the file from Sid's phone and had to make a real effort to stop herself from checking his photos and messages to Doreen.

After a few minutes, there was a quiet knock at the door. Sid had come back for his phone.

'I deleted the file,' Julia said as she held it out to him.

'Thanks for your help,' he replied with a smile, turning back to the door.

'Could you meet me at the theatre in an hour?'

'I need to swing by the station first, but I should be able to make it.'

Every now and again, Julia found that playing the cello helped her to escape from dead-end lines of thought. She had been a talented musician as a child, tackling Bach and Kodály in her early teens. Towards the end of her therapy sessions following the plane crash, she had bought a full-size cello from Philippe Dormond, and whenever she sat down to play she was always surprised by how quickly the positions came back to her.

She felt a sudden urge to take the instrument out now, to let the music carry her away, but she remained where she was, eyes on a patch of sunlight on the wall.

The old pipes clanked softly, and she heard a siren in the distance.

Lovisa had never been in Bianca's dressing room.

She hadn't set her dress on fire, hadn't tampered with her lighter.

The thought had been there all along, lurking at the back of her mind, but Julia had dismissed it as unlikely when what she should have done was give it room to breathe.

Because the fact was that the unlikely was still possible.

Only the impossible could be ruled out.

Her investigation had reached a peripeteia. Everything had been turned on its head.

She would have to start over.

There had been two unconnected perpetrators all along, and their common denominator was Bianca – and likely something else that influenced the timing.

Julia sat quietly at her desk, watching the light flickering in the leaves on the other side of the window. She took apart the chains of inference and carefully put them back together again, trying out a different order.

It was time to bring everyone together.

She was still missing a couple of keys, but before long she would have everything she needed to unlock the last few doors.

Rehearsals were due to start on the main stage at Dramaten in just over an hour's time.

Julia reached for her phone and called Bianca. The actress picked up immediately. She was on her way home from Ramon's place, walking over the Skanstull Bridge, and the wind crackled in the microphone.

'The police have arrested your stalker,' Julia told her.

She heard Bianca stop.

'Nicolás?' she asked, in a quiet, frightened voice.

'No, it—'

'Then ... then who is it?'

'It's a bit complicated, but I'll explain everything soon.'

'You're not going to tell me who's been stalking me?'

'I will, if you'll give me a couple of minutes ... I just wanted you to know that the stalker has been arrested and that the prosecutor has taken over the preliminary investigation. And I need to ask you for a favour.'

'I don't know ... You're acting kind of weird right now,' said Bianca. 'I mean, I'm the one who hired you. I'm the one who'll pay your bill.'

'And I need you to let me do things my way,' Julia explained.

'What? What do you need to do?' Bianca asked, failing to hide how irritated she was. 'You just said that the police have the stalker. That's all you were meant to be doing, that was your job, wasn't it?'

'You said you wanted the truth.'

'I do.'

'Then I need you to bring the unopened letter from Nicolás to the theatre.'

Julia heard cars racing past Bianca on the bridge, heard the wind howling in the microphone.

'I don't know . . .' she said.

'I know it's tough, but it's important. You don't have to read it yourself, but I think it might be key to getting to the bottom of everything.'

'So it's not Nicolás who has been stalking me, is that what you're saying?'

'No, it isn't Nicolás.'

'I'm so confused right now . . . You still think Nicolás was involved somehow?'

'I'm fairly confident he's dead.'

'But . . .'

'Everything will be clear soon, I promise.'

'Good.'

'Bring the letter to the theatre.'

'OK.'

Forty

J ULIA STARK PULLED ON A pale blazer over her crochet
top and set off for Dramaten. A couple of workmen who
were busy taking down some scaffolding whistled as she
passed, and a young boy was shushed by his mother when
he asked what had happened to that lady's face.

You have no idea, Julia thought.

When she got to the theatre, she stopped to wait for Sid,
leaning against her cane as she watched the people walking
along Nybrogatan. Julia moved back to make way for a reversing
van and spotted Mikko and Regina approaching the stage
entrance. The actor held out his phone to show her something,
and she gave him a playful shove before they disappeared into
the grand building.

Outside a restaurant nearby, a delivery driver was waiting
with a large pink bag on his back.

Julia saw Sid walking towards her from the metro station,
and she noticed a pretty, dark-haired woman in a yellow sundress
watching him with a longing smile.

'Tell me you saw my message,' Julia said when he reached her.

Sid held out five single-dose packs of naloxone nasal spray,
which she shoved into her bag.

'Are you going to tell me why you need naloxone?' he asked.

'Just a security precaution,' she replied with a smile.

'Do you know something I don't?'

'What I know is that you know something I don't.'

'She said, cryptically,' he muttered.

They carried eight chairs out onto the main stage and set them down around the table they would be using to rehearse the banquet scene at Macbeth's castle.

The ensemble were supposed to be having a meeting about the new casting before they got started, but Julia had spoken to Regina and told her that Bianca's stalker had been arrested, explaining that she would like to have a quick debrief with everyone first.

Julia knew her plan was slightly over-ambitious. She didn't quite know all the answers yet, but she was running out of time.

She needed to solve the case before anyone else died.

She had a number of powerful theories, and was pinning her hopes on being able to uncover the last few pieces of the puzzle as she presented her findings.

Tommy put a large thermos of coffee on a sideboard at the edge of the stage and started filling cups.

Several of the others took their seats, looking slightly confused at what was happening. Ramon set down his open can of Red Bull, draped his jacket over the back of his chair and went over to help Tommy.

Ursula came in with her thick folder and a carafe of water.

Julia's eyes were on Bianca's back. The red dress she was wearing was low-cut, one of her pink bra straps peeping out on her shoulder. The actress half-turned to Regina and showed her something.

'Ramon gave me these,' she said. With a smile, she put the two passion fruits she was holding onto a plate.

Mikko lowered the lights a little, then came out onto the stage and dumped a bag of sweets on the table.

A shiver passed down Julia's spine as she watched Sid take a pink mug of coffee from Tommy and sit down beside her.

She had no concrete proof as yet, but Julia was convinced that Kerstin Tamm had not died of natural causes. Her current theory was that the actress had drunk from a cup of poisoned coffee, causing her to stop breathing in front of everyone.

'Your soulmate,' Ramon told Ursula, passing her a mug with a picture of Franz Kafka on the side.

'Always,' she said with a smile.

Tommy put a small jug of oat milk down in front of her, and she mumbled a quiet thank you.

Mikko reached for the bag of sweets.

'OK, everyone, let's get started,' said Regina, clapping her hands and making her crystal bracelets rattle.

The others stopped talking and turned to face her.

Mikko started chewing his sweets, breathing heavily through his nose.

'I've got a question,' said Ramon. 'Are we going to vote on—'

'We'll get to that in a minute.' Regina cut him off. 'But before our meeting, Julia Stark would like a quick word.'

'Thanks,' said Julia, taking a deep breath. 'For me, this whole thing started with a simple request – to find and stop a stalker. But it turned out to be much more complicated than I could ever have imagined, and it actually involves all of you, in different ways.'

'What the hell is this?' Tommy asked with a crooked smile.

'So I'm wondering if it's OK with you, Bianca, for me to go through everything now?'

'I guess so,' Bianca replied with a shrug. 'If it's OK with everyone else?'

'Is it?' asked Julia.

'I can hardly wait,' Mikko muttered sarcastically.

Bianca reached for Ramon's Red Bull, took a sip and let out a quiet burp.

'I can't speak for everyone, but I think it could do us good,' said Regina. 'Considering the effect it's had on rehearsals so far.'

'Sure,' whispered Ramon.

'That leads me to my second question,' said Julia. 'Do you ... and above all you, Bianca, want to hear the whole truth, however uncomfortable that might be?'

'How am I meant to answer that?' she replied. 'Obviously it depends on what you're going to say.'

'Of course.'

Tommy picked up Ursula's mug by mistake, lifting it to his lips. But before he had time to take a sip, Mikko raised his voice.

'*I* want to hear the whole truth,' he said in a satisfied tone.

'Me too,' Tommy agreed, lowering the Kafka mug to the table.

'OK, fine ... if everyone else does,' Bianca said with a quick laugh.

'Bianca's stalker was arrested yesterday,' Julia began. 'Obviously I don't want to pre-empt the outcome of the legal process, but

I understand that the suspect has confessed and been remanded in custody, so I think it's probably OK for me to give my interpretation of what happened.'

'It's hard to see how that would lead to any issues of prejudice,' Sid agreed.

'The person who broke in to Bianca's apartment was Nicolás's sister, Lovisa.'

'What?' Bianca said with a frown. 'I've never even met her, as far as I know.'

'Lovisa is convinced that you've been in a long-term sexual relationship with Mikko and that you cheated on her brother with him, breaking Nicolás and meaning he stopped sleeping . . . Following the incident at Riche, which everyone here knows about, Bianca joined Nicolás on a trip to Helsinki in an attempt to save their relationship. But when she returned to Stockholm for the crisis meeting at the theatre, Nicolás's insecurities flared up again, and he drank heavily and took an overdose of sleeping pills in order to get some rest that night.'

'I didn't cheat on Nicolás,' said Bianca.

'I don't think you did either,' said Julia.

'And definitely not with Mikko.'

Ramon laughed, and Mikko slumped back with a grin.

'Yes, I know that because of what he did,' said Julia.

Mikko looked around. 'What the hell have I done now?'

'You wanted sexual favours in exchange for helping Bianca get a foot in the door here,' Julia replied.

'Is that what she told you?' Mikko asked with a cruel smile. 'Because I'm all for opening the windows and airing the dirty laundry, if that's what you want. That stuff happened a hundred years ago, but hey, what the hell. Why not.'

'Not quite a hundred years, but you're right, it was a while ago,' Julia said drily. 'And there's no doubt in my mind that it was a case of sexual exploitation ... Given how drunk Bianca was, and given the consent laws here in Sweden, it might even have been rape.'

'OK, just give it a fucking rest,' he barked. 'I could've had whoever the fuck I wanted. What the hell do you take me for?'

Julia stood up and pointed at him with her cane. 'You can leave if you don't want to hear the truth,' she said.

Forty-One

MIKKO REMAINED WHERE HE WAS, arms folded. Julia held his eye until he looked down and popped another sweet into his mouth.

She then lowered her cane, steadied herself and went on.

'No one finds you impressive, Mikko. Ask any woman, and she'll say that you're a misogynist,' she said. 'All you really want is to humiliate us and put us in our place.'

'Waa, waa,' he mumbled, trying to catch Ramon's eye.

'I don't know,' Julia continued. 'I come from a family of labourers and farmhands, and your behaviour really does remind me of *"jus primae noctis"* – you know, when the aristocracy had the right to first dibs on their workers' wives on their wedding nights.'

'I'd been to drama school,' Bianca said quietly. 'I was talented. I should have stood a chance here without having to give you a blow job in the toilet.'

Ramon was sitting quietly with his head bowed.

'The MeToo movement actually made a pretty big impact in Sweden,' said Sid. 'Except in the theatre world, which had its own hashtag: LightsCameraSilence ... All testimony was anonymous, and nothing changed.'

'Nope,' Ursula agreed in her croaky voice.

Tommy used a pen to stir some sugar into his coffee, and a droplet of the dark liquid ran down Kafka's face.

Julia's eyes panned over everyone at the table, and she saw the chains of inference crossing, breaking and reconnecting depending on who had done what. She hadn't yet managed to rule out the majority of explanations, and would need to keep studying them closely over the next few minutes.

'Mikko, you couldn't accept that Bianca had chosen someone else after she met Nicolás, that she was faithful to her fiancé. You felt manipulated, like you'd been used ... Especially after she became a star, when her name ended up above yours.'

Regina poured a little of Ursula's oat milk into her coffee and then put the jug back down on the table.

Bianca had started chewing her lower lip, and she glanced over to Ramon.

'I dunno,' said Mikko. 'I just remember Bianca being clingy and unbelievably horny.'

'You're such an old fucking perv,' Bianca muttered.

'And I remember you being unbelievably horny,' he repeated with a smile. 'I remember—'

'Honestly, go fuck yourself.' Bianca cut him off. 'I was twenty-three, you were almost fifty. I should report you to the police. It's not too late.'

'Do what you want. It'll be your word against mine,' he said with a shrug. 'Your stalker's locked up, the case is closed. Maybe we can get on with rehearsals now?'

'The stalker might be in custody, but the case is far from closed,' Julia replied calmly. 'After all, Lovisa had no way of getting into Bianca's dressing room.'

'You know it wasn't me,' said Mikko.

'That's true. I thought Mikko had been lying about his alibi because the security system had logged him as being in the same corridor as Bianca's dressing room at the time someone tampered with her lighter, but it wasn't him. I was wrong, and I've already apologised for that.'

'Apology accepted.'

'Mikko wasn't stalking Bianca, but he is undeniably guilty of other crimes like—'

'You just don't give up, do you,' he said with a smile.

'You claimed you had contacts in the underworld following the incident at Riche, and said you were going to put a price on Nicolás's head.'

'I was just trying to claw back some dignity.'

'Maybe, but you do have contacts in the underworld.'

'Do I?' Mikko smiled and gave Julia a look that was as cold as a spring brook.

'You can get hold of all the drugs you like.'

Julia's eyes drifted over the coffee cups on the table. She still wasn't sure, hadn't yet managed to put the pieces together, and kept thinking that she needed to become weightless in order to focus on the final details as time ground to a halt.

Regina took a sip of water and then moved her glass to one side. A number of angry red blotches had flared up on Ursula's throat, and Sid scribbled something in his notepad.

The director cleared her throat. 'Mikko, it was my decision to put Bianca's name above yours, because of what you did to her,' she said.

'That was a power move, to be sure,' Julia said with a sigh. 'But at the same time ... You've been doing this for years,

Regina. You knew all about what Mikko did to Bianca and continues to do to other women.'

'And you know how it works,' Regina replied. 'He's a star, he brings in the punters. I mean, if the bosses had to pick between him and me . . .'

'How do you know?' asked Julia.

'Because that's how it is.'

'OK, but from my point of view, it seems as though you chose not to kick up a fuss for your own sake, because you were scared of the effect it might have on your career.'

'Yeah,' whispered Bianca.

'You come across as conflict-shy . . . except where Tommy is concerned,' Julia continued.

'Tommy?'

'You treat him pretty badly.'

'Maybe I do, but I don't want him here,' she said. 'I just can't respect him . . . not a fucking bit, in fact.'

'Because you think he doesn't care about your daughter,' said Julia. 'But he sees her at least once a week, which is more than you.'

'Stop,' she said, turning to Tommy.

'It's true,' he said.

'Aurora told me she hasn't seen you in five years,' Regina said angrily.

'Is that why you hate me?'

'Have you been seeing her all this time?'

'Yeah, pretty much.'

'OK.' Regina sighed. 'God . . . I can't believe I fell for it again.'

'The two of you can straighten this out later, if you'd rather not have everyone else listening,' said Julia.

'She told me that you go round threatening the other homeless people unless they tell you where she is,' said Tommy. 'And that you just shout at her whenever you find her.'

'Only because I want her to give the emergency housing a chance.'

'She refuses, I know.'

'Tommy,' said Regina. 'I'm just so fucking worried, all the time. Imagine if she dies.'

'She's a grown woman and she doesn't want to come home. But maybe this winter, she says. Maybe by Christmas.'

'God ...' Regina buried her face in her hands.

Tommy leaned over and rubbed her shoulder, and she put a hand on top of his.

'I'm going to continue now, with a crucial question,' Julia said after a moment.

Bianca cut one of her passion fruits in two, reached for a teaspoon and started eating the juicy flesh.

'Man, this is delicious,' she whispered.

'Sid, there's something I need to ask you,' said Julia. 'Have you, in your capacity as a police officer, had a chance to read Nicolás's death certificate from the Finnish authorities?'

'I have,' he replied, a note of hesitancy in his voice.

'I'm fairly sure the cause of death was an overdose of fentanyl,' Julia continued.

'Stop ...' said Bianca, the colour draining from her cheeks.

Ramon turned away and stared down at the floor. Regina rubbed her face, steadying herself with both elbows on the table.

'Sid?' Julia asked. 'Am I right? I know you're limited in what you can say, but is there anything you can share?'

'Only that I genuinely have no idea how your mind works.'

'In a good sense?'

'Very good, in this case,' he said with a nod.

'OK, so Nicolás died of an overdose of fentanyl, which is an extremely potent drug. It's one hundred times stronger than morphine, which earned it the street name "drop dead" for a few years,' Julia went on.

'Nicolás wasn't a junkie,' said Bianca. 'Sorry, but I don't believe this.'

'And yet it's a fact,' said Julia. 'Which means we need to turn our attention to Ramon ... Because as Mikko gained an alibi for the time period when someone accessed Bianca's dressing room, you lost yours. Would you like to explain it yourself?'

'I don't know what you're talking about,' said Ramon, a desperate gleam in his eye. 'I haven't said anything about any fucking alibi. Why would I, when I haven't done anything wrong? I mean, obviously I've done plenty of things wrong, everyone has, but not ... not in the sense you mean.'

'Do you want some?' Bianca whispered to Sid, nodding to the second passion fruit.

'No, thanks.'

'Julia?'

'Please.'

Bianca cut through the rough outer layer and passed the plate over to Julia.

'Thank you,' said Julia, gazing out across the grand auditorium.

She desperately hoped she would start floating now, that she would be able to access her heightened state of awareness and hone in on something that would cause the entire case to crystallise and come into focus.

'I haven't touched Bianca's lighter, I swear,' Ramon said.

Julia took a sip of water, realised she had accidentally picked up Regina's glass and put it down again.

'Then what were you doing in that corridor, Ramon? Your dressing room is on another floor,' she said.

'What do you want to know?'

'Why you borrowed Mikko's key and—'

'What're you getting at?' He cut her off in a voice that was supposed to seem annoyed but actually sounded more frightened than anything.

Sid handed Julia a teaspoon, and she ate a little of the tangy fruit, crushing the seeds between her teeth and enjoying the endorphins that flooded through her veins. It almost felt as though she had just had an incredible orgasm.

Julia stretched out her legs in pleasure and splayed her toes. She had just decided that everything was going to be OK when the feeling suddenly changed shape.

Like some sort of geomagnetic reversal.

And the frightening realisation that something was terribly wrong quickly transformed into sheer panic.

'It's private,' Ramon said calmly.

Julia blinked in confusion and tried to ask Sid for help, but she couldn't manage a single word. It felt as though her body was shutting down, like she could no longer get enough air.

Her cane clattered to the floor.

She saw Sid bend down to pick it up.

As though in the distance, she heard him ask, 'Julia, what's happening?' before she stopped breathing and lost consciousness.

Forty-Two

THE RIGGING SYSTEM ABOVE THE stage creaked softly. Julia woke in the recovery position and took a deep, gasping breath. Her mouth tasted bitter, and her nostrils felt like they were on fire.

She heard Sid on the phone to the emergency services and immediately knew what had happened.

The contents of her bag had been emptied, and the stage in front of her was littered with her keys, phone, makeup, tampons and two open packs of naloxone.

Julia rolled over onto her stomach and pressed her hands to the floor.

'Just lie still,' Sid told her.

She sat up and rubbed her face hard. She then steadied herself against a chair, and Bianca helped her to her feet.

'Thank you.'

Sid opened another pack of the nasal spray as he described her condition to the call handler.

'Tell them I'm fine,' said Julia.

'There's an ambulance on its way.'

'Could I have your attention, please?' Julia asked, trying to catch everyone's eye.

'You've already got it,' said Mikko.

'We can do this tomorrow,' said Bianca. 'There's no—'

'Listen!' Julia interrupted, raising her voice. 'From now on, no one eats or drinks anything.'

'Do you mind me asking why?' asked Regina.

'Because I just survived a murder attempt, which is fortunate – not just because I'm still here, but because it gave me the final piece of the puzzle,' she said, leaning heavily on her cane.

'I don't know . . . I'm not sure about any of this,' said Ramon, looking around at the others.

'OK, maybe I wasn't quite clear enough,' said Julia. 'But let me stress how serious I am by telling you that your colleague Kerstin Tamm was murdered right here on—'

'What the hell are you saying?' asked Tommy.

'Right here on stage, in front of all of us,' she rounded off.

Regina leapt up so suddenly that her chair tipped over behind her.

'But I thought . . .' Bianca mumbled. 'I thought . . .'

'OK, you're going to have to explain,' said Regina, voice wavering. 'Are you serious?'

'I'm afraid so,' said Julia, swaying slightly.

'Do you need more spray?' asked Sid.

Regina righted her chair and walked a few steps away, studying the others like a director surveying her stage.

Mikko looked down at the table and chewed on his lower lip.

Ursula pulled her cardigan tight and shook her head almost imperceptibly.

'Julia?' Tommy pleaded.

'One of you is a murderer,' she croaked.

'And you know who?' Mikko asked, reaching for the bag of sweets and then quickly pulling his hand back.

Julia braced herself against the table as she sat down.

'Where were we?' she asked. 'Ah yes, Ramon ... We know you were near Bianca's dressing room around the time someone tampered with her lighter. I asked you why and you said it was private, but we've all agreed to tell the truth here.'

'Come off it,' said Ramon.

He attempted a smile, but his forehead was slick with sweat.

'And the truth is that you have an opioid habit,' Julia went on. 'You have for years, but you've more or less managed to keep it under wraps. Bianca knows, but she has been protecting you, which I'll come back to ... You've tried going cold turkey, but it makes you feel awful – as evidenced by the time you smashed a table using a fire extinguisher ahead of the last premiere.'

'I'd been to rehab, but I fell off the wagon,' he said quietly.

'The reason you were in the corridor by Bianca's dressing room was that Mikko had, and I quote, "hooked you up with" some synthetic opioids – Abstral this time – and you needed his private dressing room to shoot up and lie down while you waited for the high to pass.'

'I'm on top of it,' Ramon told Regina.

'I'm not sure about that,' Julia replied. 'But I am confident that you weren't the one in Bianca's dressing room ... and that you're not a killer.'

'I know,' he said.

'Of course you do.'

'And I'd be really grateful if you'd stop talking about my struggle to stay clean like it's some big fucking crime,' he said, looking at her with bloodshot eyes.

'Well said,' Julia replied. 'And I agree, I'm sorry, but your habit is actually against the law, whatever your thoughts on that . . . I wouldn't have brought it up if it wasn't important. Ramon is addicted to synthetic opioids, which means he is in touch with several dealers, and he has been trying to build up a small stockpile to avoid ever having to go cold turkey again.'

'So much drama for your money,' Mikko muttered.

'Someone else who has lost their alibi is you, Ursula,' said Julia, turning to the prompter. 'Your alibi hinged on the fact that you were in hospital, having just had an operation, the night the stalker broke into Bianca's apartment.'

'That's true.'

'Last time, you were the star acting opposite Mikko, but just before the premiere you had a severe allergic reaction. You told me all about that day, how you used a coat hanger to keep your airways open . . . And you survived, but it damaged your vocal cords.'

'Yes.'

'The rest of the cast had a crisis meeting and voted to continue with Bianca as Lady Macbeth, because she knew all your lines and cues.'

'And everyone knows how well that worked out,' Bianca muttered.

'But Ursula still felt betrayed, Bianca. You took her place and became a star, then forgot all about her . . . And now, as you all prepare to perform the same play, those old wounds have opened up again.'

'Yes.' Ursula nodded.

Julia reached for another nasal spray from Sid and put it down on the table in front of her. Her arms felt like jelly, and her heart was racing.

'During the interval of *The Seagull*, just before the final act and before the dress caught fire, Tommy went to his dressing room and noticed a bag containing a bottle of vodka outside the toilet . . .'

'Not mine,' said Mikko.

'Ursula,' said Julia. 'You recently had an operation, and your throat is still painful. You've been trying to manage that in different ways, with painkillers, throat sweets . . . And yesterday, I saw you gurgling alcohol. That was when I realised you were the second stalker.'

'I don't know what you're talking about,' said Ursula, tugging gently on her necklace.

'I'm on pretty thin ice here, but I noticed the mirror in your dressing room was streaky yesterday, Bianca, and you had a bit of lipstick on your shirt sleeve,' Julia continued with a slight gesture to her right wrist. 'My guess is that you went to your dressing room and found Ursula there, writing something in lipstick on your mirror. I don't know what, exactly, but—'

'It said, "Burn, witch. Burn",' Ursula filled in.

'Of course. Bianca was just a lowly witch originally, but she took your place,' Julia said with a nod. 'And witches are supposed to burn. Hence the dress, hence the lighter.'

'Exactly,' Ursula said with another sigh.

There was a brief silence, then Mikko started clapping.

'Thank you, but it's all a lot more . . . how can I put it . . . complicated than that,' said Julia. 'And in order to get the full picture, we need to think back to the last production. As the opening night nerves set in, the temperature rose ... Or, as Regina put it: she spat in Tommy's face, Ramon flipped out and smashed a table with a fire extinguisher, Mikko turned up drunk to the dress rehearsal, Ursula had an allergic reaction and ended up in A&E, you got absolutely panned in every review, Bianca had a breakdown, and the whole run was cancelled.'

'Don't forget the brawl at Riche,' said Regina.

'Right, Mikko tore open Bianca's blouse, Nicolás hit him and got thrown out,' Julia continued with a nod. 'Bianca then went to Helsinki in an attempt to save her relationship, and was being honest when she told Nicolás that she hadn't cheated on him. She thought she had managed to reassure him, so she came back to Sweden for the crisis meeting here and agreed to take on the female lead, only to be given the devastating news that Nicolás was dead ... And just a few days later, a letter from him arrived in the post. Bianca tried to keep it together on stage. She couldn't bring herself to open the letter, so she locked it in her safe instead. And that is where it has stayed, until now.'

'Pretty much,' said Bianca.'

'Do you have it with you?'

'Yes,' she said as she pulled it out of her bag.

'I might be wrong,' said Julia. 'But I think that letter could be the key to understanding everything ... And Bianca also clearly attached great importance to it, because she kept it safely locked away while leaving her incredibly expensive watch out in the open.'

Forty-Three

S ID PULLED ON A PAIR of gloves, got up and moved
over to Bianca to take the letter. He then returned to
his seat and sliced open the bottom edge of the envelope
using a scalpel. For a few seconds, a fine paper dust hovered
in the air around his hands.

'Bianca has asked not to hear what the letter says,' said Julia.
'Which I respect, of course.'

'It's fine, just read it,' Bianca said wearily.

'Are you sure?'

'I think so,' she replied, drying the tears from her cheeks.

'Sid, would you do us the honour?'

He carefully pulled out the letter and placed the envelope
into an evidence bag, then unfolded the sheet of paper and
cleared his throat.

'My darling Bianca,' Sid read aloud. 'I have to tell you the
truth, however hard that might be. I'm grateful for every
moment I got to spend with you, for all the love you gave me.'

Bianca let out a sob.

'That's not all,' said Julia.

'You came to Helsinki and managed to ease my mind,' Sid
continued. 'But it was too late. I couldn't tell you the truth

while you were here, but I've done something terrible and will have taken my punishment by the time you read this. You know that I'm prone to jealousy – I have no idea why, because I have no desire to control you; I know that love has to be voluntary in order to count as love.'

Bianca shuddered as another sob took hold of her, and Regina got up, walked around the table and wrapped her arms around her.

'But when I saw the two of you in Riche,' Sid read on, 'I thought you were flashing your breasts for him, that you wanted him right there and then, surrounded by everyone else ... Sorry. It's hard to write these words, but I wanted to kill you. I tried to poison you, but Ursula drank your juice instead. It wasn't an allergic reaction, like everyone thought. It was cyanide. I don't know what I was thinking. I guess I just wanted you all to myself ... Forgive me. Your Nicolás.'

'Fuck me,' Mikko muttered quietly.

Bianca dried her eyes. Her face was pale, her mascara streaky.

Ursula was sitting bolt upright, her hands in her lap, staring blankly ahead.

'God ...' Tommy mumbled.

'This is insane,' said Ramon.

'Yes ... What a twist, what a tragedy,' said Julia, forcing herself up. 'If it wasn't for the fact that the letter is a fake.'

'What?' asked Bianca. She sounded drowsy, confused.

'Let's rewind again,' said Julia, gripping her cane. 'Nicolás knew about Mikko's sexual exploitation, Bianca had been open about that from the start, and at first he thought of her as the victim she was ... He wasn't really a jealous person – he had no problem leaving his fiancée with Sonny, her

264

free-spirited ex, when he went to Brazil, for example – but everyone has their limits. And a couple of years later, during the rehearsals for the Scottish Play, when she would be acting opposite Mikko for the first time, Bianca came up with a plan ... She wanted to give Nicolás a reason to be jealous, so she made sure he saw that she had a pack of condoms in her bag when she went out to parties, she started flirting with Mikko, egging him on and letting Nicolás overhear specific fragments of phone calls, and so on ... She tried to provoke his jealousy, to push him over the edge, and ... I don't know what led to the incident at Riche, whether Bianca said or did anything to—'

'She wanted me to suck her nipples,' said Mikko.

'Never!' shouted Bianca. 'What the—'

'You said that—'

'I. Can't. Stand. You. Don't you get that?'

'Hold on, please. That's true, she can't stand you,' said Julia. 'But no matter ... Someone tore her blouse open, Nicolás saw, and he pushed his way over and hit Mikko ... He was angry and jealous, both of which could serve as motives for murder.'

'You've completely lost me now,' said Mikko.

'You were manipulated.'

'"*Fair is foul and foul is fair,*"' he quoted.

'Bianca told me she never opened the letter,' Julia continued. 'Which is true, she never did open the envelope – she sealed it.'

'Jesus Christ,' Bianca whispered, shaking her head.

'I had a hunch the first time I asked her about the letter, when she said: "I don't know, I never opened it. On the contrary ... I panicked, didn't want to know."'

'And?' Bianca asked with a laugh.

'"I never opened it. On the contrary." On the contrary would mean closing and sealing the envelope.'

'Semantics.'

'Possibly ... but on the other hand, at the time when the letter was written, only the killer knew that the juice contained kiwi. The papers hadn't published a word about an allergic reaction yet, that wouldn't break until a week later ...'

'Oof,' said Tommy, turning to Bianca.

'Bianca wanted to get Ursula out of the way once and for all, and she decided to use the tried and trusted method of cyanide poisoning,' Julia explained. 'In that context, the kiwi juice was an attempt to shield herself from any suspicion, the best possible explanation. She knew that Ursula was allergic to the fruit and that if the whole thing was simply written off as an allergic reaction then she would be in the clear. The next best solution was having someone – someone dead – who could take the rap for cyanide in case a pathologist discovered the poison.'

'You're out of your mind,' said Bianca.

'Bianca stole Ramon's fentanyl. That was why he lost it and smashed a table with a fire extinguisher.'

'I had such bad withdrawal symptoms,' he said quietly.

'She used Nicolás's computer to write the letter, then she printed it out using the hotel printer and posted it to herself here in Stockholm ... And that morning, before she left Helsinki, she swapped out his ground sleeping pills for fentanyl and made sure she was safely back in Stockholm by the time he died.'

'My God,' whispered Ramon.

'I know none of you care what I have to say, but I don't give a shit,' said Bianca. 'After everything that happened at Riche, we went home and had a huge fight ... Nicolás said that if I loved him, I'd quit acting. I wasn't even good enough to be his mistress if I followed my dreams, but I couldn't quit, I just couldn't ... I guess Nicolás knows which one I chose now, out of him and the theatre.'

'You could have just told him your choice, but he was part of a bigger plan that involved getting Ursula out of the way at the exact right moment, guaranteeing that you would be able to step into her shoes and go from a witch to Lady Macbeth,' said Julia.

'But the whole thing went to shit anyway,' Mikko said with a smile. 'She got her chance, but she couldn't stand the heat. The whole run was binned, and the theatre was left in the red.'

'I know, but when I told Sid about Bianca's breakdown on stage, he said "*Gam zu l'tova*" – the way he often does when someone has faced a setback,' Julia replied. 'It's Hebrew, and it means something like, "This too is for the best" ... Because when the production started getting bad reviews and tickets weren't selling, Bianca got a chance to act out a heartbreaking collapse on stage, to really make sure she got more opportunities going forward.'

'Which she did,' Regina said flatly.

'And the plan would have worked, too – because she eventually became a star and could have continued that way. But three years later, Regina was given a chance to stage the play again ... and she chose the same cast, largely because she was convinced that the failure last time had left a deep wound in Bianca's heart, and Bianca had almost become a second daughter to her.'

'Yes,' Regina mumbled.

'But the press release about the Scottish Play, with Mikko and Bianca reprising the lead roles, woke two sleeping lions. One was Nicolás's sister, who couldn't accept the prospect of Bianca performing opposite Mikko again, in the same play. Two people whose affair had broken her brother. Lovisa had just finished her last tour as a UN peacekeeper and returned to Stockholm ... At first, I think she just wanted to remind Bianca that she was guilty of driving Nicolás to suicide by becoming his ghost, but the power went to her head and she became a stalker. And the second sleeping lion was, as we all now know, Ursula. She had an incredibly hard time seeing Bianca take on her role again, and still felt betrayed, not realising that it was actually Bianca who had wrecked her career in the first place.'

'You really are a witch,' Ursula said in her croaky voice, pointing at Bianca.

Forty-Four

J ULIA STUDIED BIANCA FOR A moment or two. At first
glance, the actress seemed calm and composed, sitting with
a straight back and her head held high, smiling coolly at
Ursula. But her eyes were dark with stress.

'My part in all of this began when Bianca sent me a message
to say that she was being stalked by her dead fiancé,' Julia
explained. 'She genuinely believed she had seen Nicolás in the
audience during the last performance of *The Seagull* . . . That
must have come as a shock, because Lovisa really does look
like her brother. It seems Lovisa was just trying to prove a
point at first, but when she saw Bianca's reaction – she rushed
off stage – she became convinced that Bianca really had cheated
on Nicolás. The truth, however, is that her reaction had more
to do with the fact that Bianca had made a serious attempt on
his life.'

'Only an attempt?' asked Tommy.

'Until the moment she saw Nicolás in the audience, she
thought she had been successful, but was never one hundred
per cent sure,' Julia went on. 'When a diplomat dies suddenly,
the post-mortem investigation works a little differently.
Immunity, confidentiality, and so on . . . Bianca wasn't invited

to the funeral, and she never got to see the death certificate, which meant she was genuinely afraid that Nicolás was still alive and was trying to get to the bottom of what happened.'

'So is he dead?' asked Tommy.

'Yes,' Julia replied. 'Bianca tricked him into taking an overdose, and he died in a hotel room in Helsinki.'

'Goddamn,' said Ramon.

'When Sid and I first began our investigation, the plan was to work from the inside out, because whoever set fire to Bianca's dress had clearly been able to bypass the security system here,' Julia went on.

'Right.' Tommy nodded.

'We mistakenly assumed there was only one stalker, which is why we accepted Ursula's alibi right up until Nicolás's sister told us the truth. But before that, Bianca managed to catch Ursula red-handed while she was writing "Burn, witch. Burn," on the mirror in her dressing room ... She became convinced that Ursula had worked it all out and was behind everything that had happened recently. She quickly wiped the message off the mirror, because leaving it there could only harm her once she had carried out the plan that was taking shape in her mind.'

'Pretty much,' Bianca admitted.

The sound of voices and footsteps reached them from backstage, and Regina craned her neck to see who was coming.

'For all I know, Bianca really did fall for Ramon recently,' Julia went on. 'But being involved with him was also extremely convenient for her, because it gave her access to his opioids again.'

'Is that all I was to you, Bianca?' Ramon asked.

'What do you think?'

'Bianca added a few grams of the drugs to Ursula's coffee,' Julia continued. 'But as fate would have it, the cups got mixed up, and it was Kerstin who drank the poisoned coffee and died right in front of us.'

'So where are the police?' asked Mikko.

'A forensic investigation into Kerstin's death is currently underway,' said Sid.

'Until we get that report, fentanyl is just a guess, because I suspect Bianca also tested out some other poisons on the crows on her balcony,' said Julia.

'None of them worked as well,' Bianca admitted.

Sid got to his feet as two paramedics appeared with a gurney at one side of the stage. He went over to meet them and explain what was going on.

'When I came here today, I still wasn't sure who the perpetrator was, even though I already had most of the pieces of the puzzle,' Julia continued. 'They all fit in a few different ways, which meant I had three possible suspects ...'

'Brave,' Regina said with a smile.

The paramedics looked sceptical at first, but they seemed to accept the situation once Sid showed them his badge, and they then stood patiently, listening to Julia's closing words with astonishment.

'I expected the killer to make another attempt on Ursula's life,' she went on. 'So I asked Sid to bring some naloxone with him, which works as an antidote to opioids. While I was going over everything with you all, I tried to keep track of the various glasses and mugs being passed around. Ironically, I never even considered that I might be the target ... I accidentally drank some of Regina's water, but so did she ... Bianca knows that I love passion fruit, that I have an almost compulsive fondness for it, and she had injected one of them with a lethal dose of fentanyl.'

'Wow,' said Ramon.

'I'm not sure when you made up your mind to stop me,' Julia said, her eyes on Bianca. 'Was it earlier today, when we spoke on the phone, and I refused to tell you anything about the person who had been arrested? Or was it later, after Sid revealed that Nicolás died of a fentanyl overdose?'

Bianca slowly turned her head towards her and flashed her such a calm smile that Julia felt a shiver pass down her spine.

'Pretty early on, actually. I started to realise you might actually be able to solve the puzzle, as you put it. But I decided to hold off and wait. You're right, though. The thing that swung it for me was Nicolás's real cause of death. You're smart, and I realised that if you knew about that, it wouldn't be long until you put two and two together.'

'Yes.'

'I'm the one who hired you,' Bianca continued. 'So now I'm wondering ... when did you start to think that your employer might actually be involved?'

'I always do,' Julia replied. 'But aside from the fact that you wear a perfume called *Guilty*, seeing you spit into Mikko's glass was the first clue ... There was just a hint of someone capable of murder in that kind of ... how can I put it ... over-the-top act.'

'Very nice,' said Mikko.

'I also thought of the iconic scene from the Scottish Play. I mean, it's natural to shudder when Lady Macbeth imagines not being able to wash the blood from her hands, but you had a physical reaction to that moment, from the very first read-through.'

'Maybe. It almost feels like that scene was written for me,' said Bianca, shivering again.

'You just did it again,' said Julia.

'Fuck you. Seriously. I never usually misjudge people ... Now I'm sitting here, trying to work out how it can all have gone so wrong. I just wanted you to stop a fucking stalker.'

'You asked for the truth.'

'Yeah, but who really believes that means the *whole* truth?'

'The Stark Detective Agency,' Julia replied, tapping her cane against the floor three times.

Bianca reached across the table, picked up Ramon's glass and took a sip of water before anyone could stop her. She then looked at each of them in turn with a strange smile on her face.

'I was thirsty,' she said with a laugh.

'Bianca, it's not my place to come up with explanations for why you did what you did, but I have been thinking about what you went through to get a foot in the door here ... Perhaps that did more damage to your sense of self than you realised?'

'Poor little me.'

'And after that, in some dark corner of your soul, it's as though you decided you would never get anything for free,' Julia went on. 'You had to quench your own thirst ... It wasn't enough just to close your eyes and pray.'

'It never has been.'

'You'll be charged with two counts of murder and two attempted murders.'

'The police are on their way,' said Sid.

'Everyone knows not to utter the name of the Scottish Play in a theatre, and yet Bianca did it twice,' said Julia. 'That's all just superstition, of course, but it is interesting that it was *this* play ...'

'*Macbeth*,' Bianca said for a third time.

'That it was *this* play that triggered three perpetrators into action,' Julia rounded off, turning towards the paramedics.

Leaning heavily on her cane, she walked over to them and heard scattered applause behind her back as she lay down on the gurney.

Epilogue

THE EVENINGS WERE GETTING DARKER, but the days were still warm. The apple trees were laden with fruit, and faded rainbow flags continued to hang from many balconies around the city.

Stockholm's residents were all happy and sun-kissed, filled with a newfound energy. People lingered outside bars and cafés, enjoying one last glass of wine before heading home.

Julia Stark was sitting opposite Charley in a small Italian restaurant on Odengatan, having reached out to him again once the Dramaten case was over.

They were sharing a bottle of red wine and eating creamy truffle pasta. The scattered light from the enormous chandelier shifted slowly over the white tablecloth.

Charley had confessed to going on dates with two other women before giving up – until Julia got in touch again.

She had been as honest as she could be with him, explaining that because of her PTSD their relationship likely wouldn't go anywhere.

She had reached the stage where she no longer wore gloves when she saw him, but she hoped he wouldn't misinterpret that as an invitation to touch her. So far, they hadn't had any physical contact whatsoever, and had agreed that she would have to be the one to initiate it when they did.

Julia hadn't spoken to Sid since she was wheeled off the stage and admitted to hospital for observation. He had called her repeatedly at first, but she hadn't wanted to speak to him, largely because she didn't trust herself. She was afraid she wouldn't be able to handle his relationship with Doreen, afraid of ruining whatever they had – and of being unable to ask him for help again in the future.

Confidentiality prevented Julia from talking about the case with Charley, but she decided that was probably just as well, that she should try to keep her working and private lives separate going forward.

The legal proceedings against Bianca were already underway, and she was almost certain to be convicted of murder and locked away for years to come.

Regina Muhammad had been in touch to thank Julia, and had told her that she and Tommy were now living together again, giving their relationship a second chance. Her voice had faltered when she revealed that they had also started seeing their daughter together, at the centre in Hornstull.

'You know, I read Bianca's fortune before all this started,' Regina had said. 'But I couldn't show her the last card.'

'Death?' Julia guessed.

Charley topped up their glasses and explained that his architecture firm had just won a bid to design a high-rise building made entirely from wood.

He was a little older than Sid, with a furrowed brow, his skin tanned after the summer. He had tried to slick his thick hair back, and had to wear glasses to read the menu. He was wearing a blue short-sleeve shirt and a pair of dark grey chinos, had a silver ring in one ear and a child's drawing of a small family tattooed on his right bicep.

'I'm divorced with two daughters, and they live with me roughly eighty per cent of the time at the moment,' he told Julia. 'Mostly because I want to give their mum, Susanna, a bit of space. She's met a younger, better version of me – another architect, on his way up – and I can see that she's happy, which makes me happy.'

'I'm still waiting to become that mature,' Julia replied with a smile. 'I think I've already told you that I completely destroyed my last relationship, and I'm still trying to teach myself to move on, to let him go.'

'Do you have to? Because I don't want to get in the way of something that could be good again.'

'You're not in the way. Sorry, I don't think I explained that very well. I've spent more than ten thousand hours doing everything the wrong way.'

'I get what you're saying, but I don't want—'

'I'm enjoying this.' She cut him off with a smile. 'I'm glad we met, that we're sitting here, talking, eating and drinking wine.'

He nodded, put his cutlery down and gestured to the table. 'Look at us ... You know you need to move on, but your heart doesn't want to, and I've lost confidence in myself. But maybe it's time our fates took a turn for the better ... for both of us.'

Julia thought about her own fate, about the fact that she was still alive despite death having breathed down her neck so many times.

'Fate,' she whispered.

A vague hunch that both Nicolás and Kerstin had been poisoned led to her making sure she had some opioid antagonist to hand, which had saved her life when her own rush of pleasure transformed into panicked fear, when the sirens showed their true faces.

What is fate?

Three tarot cards?

The characters in *Macbeth* made destructive choices, but they were also forced to act in that way by the future that had been foretold.

In reality, fortune-telling only worked retrospectively. A person's fate simply does not exist in the present.

'I don't know,' she said. 'I'm not sure fate has anything to do with it.'

'And yet here we are, with our longing.'

Julia found herself thinking about Bianca's ex-boyfriend, Sonny. He had said that the most human behaviour of all was leaving paradise.

That was something that applied all too well to her.

She reached between the glasses, swallowed hard and lightly pressed two fingertips to the back of Charley's hand. She felt the heat of his skin and had just pulled back as though she had burnt herself when she felt her phone buzz in her bag.

Julia blushed and mumbled an apology, then looked down, dug out her phone and saw that Sid had sent her a text message.

Call me right now!